'What are yo~~u~~
Marsden?'

She titled her chin and glared at him.

'I did my escaping years ago,' she said. 'Now I've come back, and I'm rebuilding—rebuilding a real life, with a solid base and with promise for the future.

'If you don't spoil it all!' she whispered. Then she tried again to escape before he saw the tears she was desperately trying to hold back.

But he was out of his chair and moving around the table, his hand clasped like a handcuff to her wrist. So it was easy for him to haul her against his chest and wrap both arms around her.

As if it was the most natural thing in the world, she lifted her face for a kiss.

This was crazy. They hated each other.

Then the kiss blotted out all thought. The feel of Nash's lips on hers and the slow burn of desire through her body.

'We've unfinished business, Ella Marsden, and we both know it.'

Meredith Webber says of herself, 'Some ten years ago, I read an article which suggested that Mills & Boon® were looking for new medical authors. I had one of those "I can do that" moments, and gave it a try. What began as a challenge has become an obsession, though I do temper the "butt on seat" career of writing with dirty but healthy outdoor pursuits, fossicking through the Australian Outback in search of gold or opals. Having had some success in all of these endeavours, I now consider I've found the perfect lifestyle.'

COMING HOME
FOR CHRISTMAS

BY
MEREDITH WEBBER

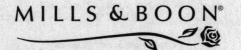

MILLS & BOON®

First published in Great Britain 2005
Harlequin Mills & Boon Limited,
Eton House, 18-24 Paradise Road, Richmond, Surrey TW9 1SR

© Meredith Webber 2005

ISBN 0 263 84343 2

Set in Times Roman 10 on 11 pt.
03-1105-55980

Printed and bound in Spain
by Litografía Rosés, S.A., Barcelona

CHAPTER ONE

GUILT gnawed at Nash as he drove into Edenvale. It had been four—or was it five?—months since he'd been home. That long since he'd seen his mother.

Not that she complained. As long as he kept in touch with weekly phone calls, she seemed content.

But, then, his mother never complained about anything. Not about the loneliness he knew she'd felt since his father had died. Not about her heartache over the loss of his brother, Russell. Not about the pain of the arthritis that had swollen her pianist's fingers into reddened ugliness. Not even about the lack of grandchildren he guessed she longed for...

'I suppose you'd call it a pretty town.'

Karen's comment wasn't a compliment to Edenvale—more a put-down. Edenvale's prettiness being the only thing it had going for it, in her opinion.

'It's a great town,' Nash said quietly, remembering the freedom of his childhood in this little haven beside the sea. Remembering friends, and adventures, and the deep abiding love for the place that he'd always believed would draw him back eventually, to take over the practice that had been his father's, and his grandfather's before that.

'Getting bigger, too,' Karen continued. 'I phoned a real-estate agent down here yesterday. He said the price of beach-front property in the district has sky-rocketed, but it'll go even higher in a couple more years as more wealthy investors real-ise the potential. I do hope you can persuade your mother not to sell.'

Me, too!

The thought startled him. For the first time since his mother had phoned to say she was thinking of selling the practice, he had made a decision. Until now, he had dithered about whether or not the practice mattered to him any more. And Nash was not a man that dithered. One of the things that made him such a good A and E doctor was his ability to make quick and effective decisions.

But dither he had! He'd wondered whether it was worth holding onto the practice for a little longer, not because it would be worth more money in a couple of years but in case he finally decided to return to Edenvale—to live out the dream of his childhood.

The 'me, too' had told him the dream must still be lodged somewhere in his subconscious—not completely obliterated by Karen's continual nagging that he specialise in dermatology, or by his own occasional desire to learn more A and E skills and perhaps go on to become an intensivist.

He turned onto the promenade, letting down his car window to breathe in the salt-laden air, driving slowly now as the slosh of the small waves and the sparkle of sunlight on blue-green water filled his soul with a sense of home.

The silly words 'me, too' echoed in his head, but they had more strength and urgency this time.

Did he really think he might come back to Edenvale permanently?

Karen was still talking about the property market. He glanced towards her, knowing he'd lose her if he did choose to come home…

Wondering if he'd care…

'I think I need a couple of good nights' sleep,' he muttered, unable to believe the direction his thoughts were taking. He and Karen had been seeing each other for four years. She was expecting an engagement ring for Christmas. He knew that because she'd left glossy magazines, open at ads for expensive diamonds, all around his apartment.

For a non-ditherer, he'd been dithering a lot over Karen, too…

'Well, that's not going to be possible this weekend,' she said cheerfully. 'We've got the Beavises' party tonight and the opening of Charlie's art exhibition tomorrow. It really wasn't the best weekend to be visiting your mother.'

Nash accepted the mild rebuke, knowing Karen had been very forbearing about the string of weekends he'd worked over the last few months, and very reluctant about this trip to Edenvale on the first weekend of his four weeks' leave.

Though, of course, she hadn't had to come. He'd told her that.

And now, as he drove up along the road that wound around the headland, towards the house where he'd grown up, he cravenly wished she wasn't with him so he could indulge in the feeling of homecoming and let remembrance lap about him and enfold him without guilt or embarrassment.

He turned into the drive, seeing the house ahead—wide steps leading up to an even wider veranda, the front door set back under the eaves, a dog standing—

A dog?

His mother had a dog?

And not just any dog, but a tall, lean, graceful dog.

A greyhound!

'Sarah must have visitors,' Karen said, 'though why visitors would bring their dog when they come to call, I don't know. They must realise her mobility is compromised by her arthritis. A dog like that could knock her over.'

Nash stopped the car at the bottom of the steps. The dog had a look of belonging about it. Not a visiting dog at all.

The child who appeared from the shadows behind the dog looked equally at home. She was a child from a picture book—golden brown curls escaping from a red ribbon tied around her head, chubby pink cheeks, a rosebud of a mouth and clear wide eyes looking enquiringly at them.

She was also familiar somehow...

'See, visitors,' Karen was saying as she got out of the car.

The little girl moved closer to the dog and put her arm around its neck, having to stretch up just a little to do it.

'Sarah's in the shower and she said to tell you to come around the back.'

The words were run together in the manner of a message repeated often so as not to be forgotten.

'Thank you for telling us,' Nash said, moving close enough to see the hazel colour of the child's clear wide eyes. 'Are you visiting Sarah?'

She studied him for a moment. Checking to see if he deserved an answer to his question.

'I was getting Girlie for her bath.'

Her clear hazel eyes and a certain tilt of her head reminded him of someone yet he couldn't place the resemblance—and he *knew* he didn't know the child.

'Is this Girlie?'

Beside him, Nash could feel Karen's impatience building, but the beautiful child and the nudge of memory held him in thrall.

The child nodded.

'And I'm Brianna,' she announced, then held out her spare hand towards Nash.

He took the slightly grubby offering and shook it solemnly.

'I'm Nash,' he said. 'I'm Sarah's son, and this is Karen.'

'Is Karen your girlfriend?'

'Let's go in,' Karen said, before Nash could work out why he hadn't wanted to answer the question.

Of course Karen was his girlfriend!

'Oh, there you are. I'm sorry. I meant to be here to greet you, but Girlie wanted to play and that made me late with my shower. I hope Brianna explained.'

His mother came around the side of the house, looking so well and moving so freely Nash found himself staring in disbelief. Then he scooped her into his arms and gave her a huge hug.

'Look at you!' he said, releasing her to hold her at arm's length. 'You look great!'

He took her hands and inspected them.

'No redness, no swelling! You've found some magic elixir for curing arthritis. Share the secret and we'll all be rich.'

Sarah chuckled.

'Not a magic elixir but a new doctor who's stubborn enough never to give up.'

She extracted one hand from his and offered it to Karen.

'Karen, lovely to see you. Do come around the back, the pair of you.'

'Around the back? Are you working in the garden?' Karen asked the question as her high heels pecked their way along the gravel path, following Sarah, the child and the dog.

Nash walked behind, disturbed in some way he couldn't define. By the child's resemblance to someone?

By this trek around the house?

'I'm sorry, I should have explained.' His mother had halted by a new green plastic water tank near the back steps. 'I've been in the little house for so long now I didn't think to tell you I'd moved.'

'Moved? Out of your glorious house? Where to?' Karen must then have worked out the answer for herself, for she continued, in horrified tones, 'Not into the locum's cottage?'

Sarah laughed.

'You make it sound as if I've shifted to a slum or squat. It's a lovely house, much more modern than the old place, and now the pines have grown so tall in the garden, it has a far better sea view. It's also a better size for me. I was rattling around in the old place—feeling lost and lonely. The little house closes around me—makes me feel secure.'

She paused, then touched the dog's head.

'The house and Girlie both.'

Nash shook his head, but guilt was gnawing at him once again. How could he not have known this? Had his mother told him and he'd forgotten, or had he not always listened properly when he'd phoned, not from love but from duty?

Or had she not told him?

And if not, why not?

Suspicion was a much easier companion than guilt, and he was about to ask why this little matter hadn't been mentioned earlier when a light, high laugh came from behind the rock wall of the kitchen garden, then three more lean, graceful dogs appeared, followed by a woman so like the child Nash could only stare at her. Long legs flashed beneath cut-off denim shorts faded to the pale chalky blue of the sky in summer, while a sodden T-shirt clung lovingly to full breasts. The curls were the same, although they appeared to be held back not by a red ribbon but by red tape—the pink stuff much favoured in legal offices.

'Oh!'

Confusion or embarrassment brought a rush of colour to her cheeks, making her look ridiculously young.

And so familiar he could barely breathe.

But it couldn't be Ella—not in his mother's back yard.

With dogs?

Dogs! Meg was a vet—maybe it was Meg!

And though his heart knew it was Ella, hope had him saying a tentative, 'Meg?'

He saw the lovely face tighten at the same instant he remembered. Meg was dead. Killed by a drug addict at the veterinary practice where she'd worked. That was one thing his mother *had* told him.

Ella was a doctor…

Now too many answers fell into place in his brain. The sense of familiarity when he'd seen the child, and Sarah's silence on her move to the locum's cottage…

'I'm Ella Marsden,' Ella was saying, apparently to Karen as he certainly needed no introduction to the second of the Marsden twins. 'I won't shake hands. I'm covered in this revolting goo. It's supposed to be an effective but non-chemical method of keeping fleas off the dogs but I think all it's going to do is make living with them enormously unpleasant. I'm sure you can smell it on me.'

She clicked her fingers and the dog named Girlie went to her.

'Would you excuse me? I've just time to wash Girlie, too, before morning surgery starts. I thought I'd be done before you got here. I didn't expect city doctors to be up and about this early. Come on, Brianna. We'll get out of Sarah's way.'

With a slight motion of her head that might or might not have been an acknowledgement of Nash's presence she walked away.

Nash glanced towards his mother and saw a little frown plucking at her eyebrows, then her eyes met his, pleading for understanding—for him to at least listen before he exploded.

Fat chance!

'*That* was Ella Marsden!' he stated, aiming for icy control but practically stuttering with fury.

'Do you know her?' Karen had obviously missed the escalating tension in the atmosphere, but she could hardly miss the glare Nash turned on her.

'Stay out of this, Karen,' he growled, in case she *had* missed it. Then he turned to his mother. 'Tell me you're not thinking of selling the practice to Ella Marsden! Tell me she's not the reason you've moved out of your home! Have you gone out of your mind?'

'Nash, you can't speak to your mother that way!'

Karen's protest was lost in his mother's calm, 'Let's go into the cottage and discuss this like adults, Nash, without the histrionics.'

'Histrionics? Histrionics?' Nash *was* spluttering now! 'After all they've done to our family, you want to sell my father's practice to a Marsden! And I'm not allowed to be upset?'

You shouldn't have made that crack about city doctors, Ella told herself as she led Girlie to the tub she'd set up in the back yard. Her heart was pounding, her stomach churning and her knees so shaky she was surprised they were holding her upright.

She hadn't even said hello to him, and he'd take that as a deliberate snub. How else could he possibly take it?

But if only for Sarah's sake she wouldn't have snubbed him—she just hadn't been able to find the air to form his name, then had gulped in replenishment and yammered away at his girlfriend, making a total idiot of herself.

She'd been dreading this meeting with Nash McLaren.

Returning to Edenvale had been hard—on so many levels—but during the five months she'd been here she'd worn away at the locals' prejudice, gradually winning respect if not affection from the majority of them.

And she'd begun to believe everything would be all right.

Then suddenly Nash had been there, right there in front of her, and seeing him—tall, strong-looking, and impossibly handsome—had tied her tongue in knots and started flutters in her stomach that she hadn't felt since she'd been fifteen.

They had to be a kind of delayed hangover from those days.

She couldn't possibly still harbour feelings for Nash McLaren.

The look he'd given her should have killed even the strongest flutter. It had certainly told her she had no hope of winning *his* approval, though she'd guessed that from the beginning. But recently it had bothered her less, mainly because her opinion of *him* had sunk lower than even she'd thought possible. Five months and the rat had not once made the two-hour journey from the city to see his mother!

And how, as a doctor, he could have let his own mother's arthritis get as bad as Sarah's had been—well, Ella didn't know. What she did know was that just thinking of Nash McLaren made her blood boil.

Still!

She was listing her grievances against the man in an attempt to overcome the mortification she felt at him seeing her at her utter worst. Wet, bedraggled, smelling of—well, the closest polite description would be a sewage pond, while he stood there in his smart casual clothes, with his equally smart girlfriend, the two of them eyeing her as if she was of less importance than an earwig.

Damn him *and* his smart girlfriend!

And damn the past for intruding into her life right now. But the sight of Nash, all grown up but still as gorgeous as he'd been at eighteen—had taken her straight back to that terrible time—to her fifteen-year-old self sobbing in Meg's arms, not because their father had died but because Nash McLaren, the boy to whom she'd lost her vulnerable teenage heart, had dropped her for Lisa Warren, a ditzy blonde bombshell who had carved notches in her ruler for all the boys she'd kissed.

'Are we going to wash Girlie?' Brianna asked.

Ella looked at the little girl—Meg's daughter—and found a smile.

'I think maybe we'll leave her until tomorrow,' she said, then, ignoring the state of her smelly clothes, she swung her niece into her arms and gave her a tight hug. 'Let's go into the house and have a shower, then you can help Mrs Carter make the scones for Sarah's morning tea while I go to work.'

'Can I go to Sarah's morning tea?'

'I don't know, poppet. Maybe Sarah wants Nash all to herself this morning.'

'But that other lady's there.'

Irrefutable child logic.

'She's his girlfriend—they apparently come as a matched set,' Ella said, then instantly regretted the bitchy remark. There was no need to poison Brianna's life with her own bitterness.

'If Sarah asks you, you can go,' she said, walking around the veranda to the bathroom then depositing her precious cargo on the floor.

They showered together, a messy business which Brianna always felt was a great treat. Once both of them were dressed, Ella led the little girl through to the kitchen.

Mrs Carter bustled forward, wrapping an apron around Brianna's tiny waist then lifting her 'helper' onto a stool. The hard, hot lump of anger that had been building in Ella's heart melted. There were too many positives in this situation—the best being the love Mrs Carter and Sarah both lavished on Brianna—for her to let her antagonism towards Nash ruin it for them. He didn't want the practice—Sarah was certain of that—and while he might not want his mother to sell to Ella, it would be Sarah's decision in the end.

Ella felt just the smallest twinge of conscience, knowing it was Sarah's affection for Brianna that might weight the decision in her favour if Nash did argue. But it wasn't as if she had deliberately used her niece. Brianna had won Sarah's heart—and Mrs Carter's—simply by being her sunny, loving, lovely self.

'Old Crosspatch is here!'

Kate, Ella's weekend receptionist, greeted her with this unwelcome news. 'Old Crosspatch' was the former mayor of the town, and one of the least admiring of Ella's patients. But Ella forgave him a lot as his body was now racked with the tremors of Parkinson's disease, and he had trouble articulating all the thoughts of his still active and acute mind.

'Come on through, Mr Warburton,' Ella said, leading the way from the waiting room to her office but being careful not to offer help she knew would be refused.

'Don't know why your office has to be so far from the reception,' he grumbled as he followed her shakily along the corridor.

'The others are examination rooms,' she said, although she knew he knew that. 'Though I've been thinking, if I buy the place, I might change the set-up and put my office closer.'

'Doug McLaren knew what he was doing, so I wouldn't be too hasty to change things, young woman.'

Ella stifled a sigh. It was always this way—no matter what she said to Mr Warburton, she was wrong.

'So, what can I do for you today?' she asked, when he was finally seated in her consulting room. At least she'd learned not to ask him how he was—that had always brought on a derisive tirade about how the hell she thought he might be, with his life shaking away from him.

'Well, I don't want you poking and prodding me or taking my blood pressure. You did all that on Wednesday. But you talked about that new drug,' he grumbled, and Ella forgot her past grievances with this man in her excitement that maybe, just maybe, he'd listened to her at his most recent appointment.

'Not so much a new drug as the use of an antidepressant as part of your treatment,' Ella reminded him.

'Tell me again—about the things my body isn't producing now. I'm not depressed but you said I could be lacking in some of those things.'

Ella didn't smile, understanding where Mr Warburton was coming from. In his mind, depression would be a sissy thing for a man to suffer, but chemical depletion—well, that would be all right.

'Parkinson's affects the brain cells that tell the body to produce things like serotonin and norepinephrine, which are two chemicals that help you feel mentally well balanced and good about yourself.'

She eyed her patient, wondering if she'd phrased it in a manner acceptable to him.

He nodded, and relief released her tense muscles.

'Then it seems stupid not to take something that will re-place what the body's not producing.' Mr Warburton said, and Ella drew her prescription pad towards her. As a doctor she should be—and was—glad that Mr Warburton had agreed to try something to alleviate the depression up to fifty per cent of Parkinson's patients suffered from, but as a person she was happiest for Mrs Warburton, who had borne the brunt of her husband's anger at the disease which was taking over his life.

'I was reading of some new tests undertaken in the US and Europe,' she told him as she passed the script across. 'I'll get all the information together for you and you can decide if you'd be interested in trying it. Not a tablet, but a patch, so drugs are fed into your body through the skin. Apparently it helps with the "downtime" you suffer on the normal drugs.'

Mr Warburton nodded at her, then surprised her by saying, 'Heard Nash was due to visit Sarah today.' He studied Ella for a moment then added, 'He coming back where he belongs at last?'

'I don't know,' Ella said, although his question had quashed the little bit of joy his acceptance of the antidepressants had given her.

Of course the older residents of the town would rather have Nash as their doctor. In country towns the local doctor was still part of the elite and as the son and grandson of the town's previous GPs, Nash certainly had the pedigree. Who did she, daughter of the town drunk and a cheat to boot, think she was to aspire to that exalted position?

But right now she needed to be here if she was to pursue the dream she and Meg had shared from their teenage years— a dream that was now hers alone to achieve.

She followed Mr Warburton back down the corridor, her confidence sunk so low it was all she could do to smile at the next patient. Though when she saw who it was, her smile became genuine. Carrie Mills had cerebral palsy, but a gamer, feistier, more determined four-year-old Ella had yet to meet.

Ella's smile became a frown as she realised Carrie hadn't replied to her greeting with a smile and a wave of her good hand. Carrie was slumped in her mother's arms, and Jenny Mills was looking at Ella with desperate, pleading eyes.

'She's got this rash,' she whispered, and Ella knew she wanted reassurance. Wanted the rash to be measles or chickenpox, although Carrie had been immunised against both.

Maybe a heat rash…

'Let me take her,' Ella said, lifting the sick little girl from her mother's arms, knowing she could look at the patches of reddened pinpricks on her pale skin as she carried her— knowing also that if it was the dangerous meningococcal rash, then the sooner Carrie was in hospital the better.

Once again she cursed the fact that Edenvale hospital had been closed ten years ago. If there were two doctors in town, it could be reopened. She'd never seen a meningococcal rash, but in a hospital she could have tested Carrie's spinal fluid, and if it *was* meningococcal could have started her on treatment straight away, without the drama of a two-hour trip to the city and disruption of the family's life.

She set the little girl down on the examination table and looked at the pinprick spots on her face. They looked like the photos she'd seen of meningococcal rash, and she couldn't think of anything else that would produce a rash like it. A rash and fever—Carrie was hot to the touch. But she couldn't be certain, she knew she would need a second opinion but time was of the essence.

Nash worked A and E—Nash would know!

The thought came out of nowhere and brought a new flicker of anxiety down her spine, not for her patient but for herself. She'd made a total hash of their meeting this morning and now she'd be asking for his help.

Oh, for heaven's sake, Ella, this isn't about you, it's about Carrie. It's about the child's survival—and the man would have experience of the disease...

She waited until Jenny sat down, then handed Carrie back to her and, with shaking hands and a heavy heart, lifted the phone.

'Kate, could you put me through to Sarah, please?'

It took only seconds, and it wasn't Sarah but the man she wanted who answered the phone.

'Nash McLaren.'

'Nash, it's Ella. I'm really sorry to bother you but I need your advice. Sarah tells me you've been working A and E. Have you seen much meningococcal—early stage—rash? I've a vulnerable patient here—four-year-old with CP—and if it is meningococcal I'd like to start penicillin G now rather than wait until she gets seen in a city hospital.'

'Could be hours before she's seen in hospital,' Nash agreed. 'I'll be right there.'

'Nash McLaren?' Jenny asked. 'Don't tell me he's finally turned up to visit his mother?'

'Be nice, Jenny,' Ella warned, bending over the little girl and taking her temperature with an ear probe. 'He's a specialist A and E doctor. He's trained to detect early symptoms and that could make all the difference to Carrie's recovery.'

'For that, I'll be nice,' Jenny promised, 'but I won't forgive him for the way he treats his mother, especially when you consider what she's been through. He used to be fun, but he got altogether too big for his boots when he went off to university. Too high and mighty for Edenvale. He didn't even come to our ten-year high-school reunion.'

'Maybe coming back is painful for him. He and Russell were closer than a lot of brothers and it's less than five years since Russell died.'

Ella wasn't sure why she was making excuses for him when she'd been as mad as hell at him herself.

'I hadn't realised you were in his year,' she added, wishing the past didn't raise its head so often in conversation with patients. But thankfully the talk stopped there, for Nash knocked once on the door then opened it, seeming even taller—and even better-looking—than he had when Ella had seen him earlier.

'Hi, Nash. Jenny Mills—Jenny Roberts that was.'

It was a good thing Jenny introduced herself, because Ella had lost all the air from her lungs again.

'Jenny Roberts?' Nash smiled at Jenny. 'Now Jenny Mills. So you *did* marry Josh! Good on you.'

He was kneeling by Jenny's side, talking easily, but Ella could see all his attention was on Carrie.

'And who's this gorgeous young woman?'

'This is Carrie,' Jenny said, her antagonism to Nash already gone, swept away by his effortless charm.

But some of Ella's antagonism was also swept away, only for her it was because of the gentle way he handled Carrie, holding her hand and talking to her all the time he was examining her, treating the little girl with immense dignity.

'I think you're right,' he said, standing up and turning so he could speak to both Ella and Jenny. 'She should go straight to Sydney, but in an ambulance so she can be monitored on the way. We'll start the drugs—you have some?' He broke off to turn to Ella who nodded. 'Good. Now, Jenny, is Josh at home? Can he pack some things for you and Carrie and meet you here? You can go in the ambulance with her. Do you have other children?'

'Pete can come and stay with me,' Ella offered, remembering that both Josh's and Jenny's parents were holidaying on the Gold Coast at the moment. Jenny nodded, though she was looking shell-shocked at how fast things were moving. 'I'll get Kate to phone for the ambulance then phone Josh for you.'

Ella left the room, wanting to get the penicillin for Carrie and to tell Kate what was happening—but also for a little breather away from Nash. Since he'd been there, in the office that had been his father's, she'd felt breathless and disorientated—her usual efficiency marred in some way by her reaction to Nash.

Surely anger couldn't manifest itself in breathlessness…

She found the drug she wanted and a bag of fluid. A quick pinch of the skin on the back of Carrie's hand had shown she was already dehydrated, and the drug would work faster through an IV infusion. What else did she need?

'Do you have a supply of vaccine?'

She turned to find Nash had joined her in the storeroom.

'Vaccine?' she echoed stupidly. 'It's too late for that, Nash.'

He gave her the earwig look again.

'For her brother and other children with whom she's been in contact. Jenny tells me Carrie goes to preschool. I know it doesn't spread easily from physical contact, but with kids sharing toys and probably towels, the other children in her class should all be vaccinated as soon as possible.'

I'd have thought of that next, Ella muttered internally, defensive in the face of Nash's implied criticism.

'I've got some supplies of the A and C vaccine on hand as we've recently done all the first-year high-school kids. People don't realize that after infants, teenagers seem to be the most at risk. I've been trying to persuade all parents to consider immunisation, even if they have to pay for it.'

'I imagine the cost is prohibitive for some families.'

He was following her back to the consulting room where two ambulancemen were already strapping Carrie to a stretcher.

'I've offered a pay-by-the-month scheme to people who can't afford it, but it's such a rare thing it's hard to convince parents to take that option.'

Ella turned her attention to Carrie, telling the sick little girl what she was doing and explaining she'd have to go back to the hospital for a while.

No stranger to hospital, Carrie accepted it, though Ella guessed the child was too sick to know what was happening. Josh arrived as they were loading Carrie into the ambulance. He had a bag in one hand and was clutching five-year-old Pete with the other. And although his eyes were filled with pain as he looked at his daughter, he remained calm, kissing Jenny goodbye, assuring her he'd drive carefully and see her at the hospital, then giving Pete a hug.

'You be good for Ella and Sarah and Mrs Carter,' he said, and the bright-eyed boy nodded agreement.

'That'd be OK if he had any concept of the word "good",' Ella heard Kate, who'd come out to watch the departure, whisper.

But Josh had realised Nash was there, and as the ambulance drove off the two were talking, Nash reassuring Josh everything that could be done would be done, Josh saying he hoped they'd have time to catch up with each other some time soon. So it was to Nash he passed his son, and Ella, who'd hated the enthusiasm of the exchange of memories—the last thing she wanted right now was for Nash to think he might enjoy returning to Edenvale—had to admit Nash behaved beautifully to the little boy, squatting down to talk to him about how fast the ambulance could go.

Man talk!

'I gather, from what Josh said, Pete has stayed with you before.' Nash rose to his feet, silvery blue eyes meeting and holding Ella's.

'Carrie's been hospitalised a lot lately. First she had an op to release tight tendons in her left ankle and since then a series of chest infections have had her in and out of hospital. One or other set of grandparents used to take him, but both grandfathers have recently retired and they've been travelling a lot. SKI holidays.'

Nash frowned at her.

'Ski holidays? It's midsummer.'

Ella grinned.

'Not that kind of ski—the other kind. Don't tell me you haven't heard of retirees' SKI holidays—the SKI stands for Spending the Kids' Inheritance.'

The frown on Nash's face didn't lessen much, though it seemed more directed at her than at retirees' SKI holidays.

Maybe she shouldn't have smiled at him, tried to lighten the atmosphere between them.

She turned her attention to Pete, who'd wandered away from Nash and was now poking a spider's web with a small stick.

'Come on inside, Pete,' she said. 'Kate will find you some toys to play with, then I'll take you across to the house to play with Brianna and the dogs when I finish with my patients.'

'If Pete's going over to the house, I can take him,' Nash offered, and though Ella knew Kate would be more than happy to have him out of the reception area, she also knew she couldn't expect Mrs Carter to cope with both children *and* morning tea for the visitors.

'No, he'll be fine here,' she said, and took Pete's hand to lead him inside.

Nash's frown was back, but Pete had escaped her clutches and was dashing into the reception area, so Ella had no time to worry about the frown. An unrestrained Pete Mills could wreck a room in two minutes flat, and the patients in the waiting room would only sit and watch. Like the Marsden twins in the past, Pete Mills already had a reputation for being wild!

CHAPTER TWO

DID she not trust him with the child?

Annoyed by what had seemed to be a dismissal, Nash followed Ella back into the waiting room, in time to see her swoop on the child as he lunged towards the water-cooler.

'I'll get you a drink, Pete,' she said, holding him firmly with one hand and extracting the five paper cups he'd pulled from the dispenser from his grip.

'ADHD?' Nash queried, as, with him still following, she led the little boy around behind the high reception counter.

'More like attention-seeking, in my opinion,' Ella replied, sitting Pete down at a small table in the corner of the reception area. It must have been a common occurrence as the receptionist was rummaging in a cupboard and now crossed the room with a plastic box filled with wooden puzzles.

'Are you going to give him rifampicin as a prophylactic?'

Ella was bent over the table, setting out a puzzle for the little boy.

She straightened up and looked Nash in the eye, raising one eyebrow by way of reply.

A very expressive eyebrow, telling him he was out of order and what she did was none of his damn business. Unfortunately, as well as telling him that, it reminded him of the past—of a hot summer day not long before he'd left Edenvale to go to university when he'd come across her unexpectedly, out near the caves. She'd seen him coming and, sure she'd avoid him, he'd called to her to wait. But once he'd reached her, he hadn't been able to find the words he'd wanted to say, and, instead of trying, he'd kissed her. Kissed her until they'd both been breathless!

Eventually, she'd pushed a little away from him and raised that eyebrow.

'Do you kiss Lisa Warren like that?' she'd asked, then she'd walked away without waiting for an answer.

She was talking to the receptionist, Kate, asking her to phone people who had appointments later in the morning, telling them she was running behind time. More consideration than a lot of GPs showed.

He'd turned his mind from past breathless kisses and was reluctantly considering just how good a GP she might be when he realised she was talking to him.

'Pete's been vaccinated with the bivalent A and C polysaccharide vaccine. Of course, it won't provide protection against group B meningococcal disease, or any of the other strains they're finding now, if Carrie proves to have one of them, but as far as my reading goes, group C is the most likely.'

She frowned and for no reason at all he had an urge to tell her not to worry.

Stupid, of course. She was all the town had in the way of a doctor—she *had* to worry!

'But, then,' she continued, 'the consensus is that outbreaks are more common in winter or spring, not midsummer, so I can't keep thinking of the norm. But, as far as Pete's concerned, one of the local service clubs raised the funds for us to vaccinate all the children starting school next year, so he's covered if it's A or C. Carrie's in the year behind Pete at preschool and would have been vaccinated because of her vulnerability but she was in hospital at the time we were doing it, then with her chest problems not fully resolved, it didn't seem wise…'

Now cocky Ella Marsden was showing some doubt! He should have been delighted, but found himself unexpectedly moved by the worry in her eyes. Clear hazel eyes framed by dark lashes that seemed more mesmerising because she'd hauled her tumble of curls into some kind of order, pinning the mass of them in a coil at the back of her head.

'No one would vaccinate a child who was already ill,' he said, but it was too late to offer reassurance. After a word of warning to Pete to behave, she'd whisked out the door, called to a patient and was striding down the corridor towards her office.

'I assume you're Sarah's son.'

He turned to find Kate watching him—watching him watch Ella.

He nodded, then realised his manners had gone missing and introduced himself.

'Don't suppose you're looking for a job?' Kate asked. 'This place needs an extra doctor. Ella's running herself into the ground.'

An image of Ella as he'd first seen her that morning rose unbidden in his mind. She'd looked so fresh and young and wholesomely attractive, he had to doubt the receptionist's words, but Kate had already turned away to answer the phone so he couldn't question her.

The town was growing—all the towns along the coast were—and they were especially busy over the summer holidays when people flocked to spend Christmas at the beach. But if Edenvale had become a two-doctor town, was his mother asking enough for the practice?

Nash groaned in his head. Four years of dating Karen and he was thinking like her. Even though his father had lost money in the co-op debacle, his mother was comfortably off. She didn't need to sell the practice for financial reasons. He earned a good income and didn't need a handout, so why would the price of the practice matter?

He must have stood there for longer than he'd realised because now Ella was back, already seeing one patient out and calling the next to come through to her room.

Without bothering to analyse his reasons, Nash took the chair opposite Pete at the play table and began to talk to the little boy and help him with his puzzle. The phone rang constantly.

'Yes, he's here, Sarah. No, the emergency's over but he's keeping Pete Mills occupied for us.'

He and Pete had just completed a complicated jigsaw with a barnyard theme and Pete was pointing out all the animals in the picture when Kate's conversation impinged on Nash's concentration.

Damn! He'd come to Edenvale to visit his mother—what on earth was he doing, playing with a child?

'Sarah said to take Pete up to her place—she's fixing lunch in the garden and he loves playing there.'

'Lunch?'

Kate grinned at him.

'It's just after midday. I had a feeling you were enjoying that puzzle as much as Pete was.'

Nash frowned at her then glanced towards the waiting room, which didn't seem any emptier than it had been when he'd first come in.

'When does surgery finish?'

Kate smiled again.

'Eleven o'clock—or that's what it says on the door. But today we'll be lucky if we're done by two, and when you consider Ella only sees emergency cases on Saturdays, you might understand why we need two doctors.'

Nash thought back to what his mother had said—when he'd calmed down sufficiently to listen to her!—something about Ella wanting to buy the practice so she could take in a partner.

Her daughter's father perhaps?

Now, why would he think that?

'Come on, Pete, we'll go up to—'

'He calls her Sarah—all the children do.'

Nash turned to find Ella standing on the other side of the reception counter.

'Going to Sarah's!' Pete said happily, taking Nash by the hand and dragging him towards the door.

But uneasiness dogged Nash's footsteps as he went with the boy—past Ella, who was speaking to a patient, through the door and up the drive, around the big house and towards the cottage. All what children called his mother Sarah?

More to the point, why?

He couldn't recall his mother ever having much to do with the children of Edenvale, though she'd thrown fabulous birthday parties when he and Russell had been children. But his mother's good works had been concentrated on the hospital guild, and when that had closed... What had she done with her time?

He was ashamed to say he had no idea.

Ella breathed a sigh of relief as the pair disappeared from view. Although Nash had been behind the reception counter she'd been conscious of his presence in the surgery every time she'd walked into the waiting room.

Was he checking up on her? Was that why he'd stayed and played with Pete?

Or was he counting the patients she saw in an hour so he could tot up how much she'd have to pay his mother for the practice?

Well, he was more than welcome to look at the books, but she and Sarah had already agreed on a price. Two prices, in fact. One for the practice and another for the surgery building and the big house. Ella desperately wanted the latter option, knowing she'd be securing Brianna's future if she could buy the property, but the banks were reluctant to lend money to a single woman, and she doubted she'd find one kind enough to lend her such a vast amount.

She had savings, of course, but most of those were already earmarked...

Setting aside her financial worries for the moment, she called in her next patient. Five to go—that's if no one else arrived. She should be done by two—three at the latest—but one look at Jessie Cochrane's face told her finishing any time soon wasn't going to be possible. The little girl had the same petechial rash—the tiny red burst blood-vessel spots—Carrie had had. Same class at preschool—same class as Brianna.

Gently she examined the child, explaining to Libby, Jessie's mother, what was happening. Jessie's temperature was elevated, her neck was stiff and the rash told its own story. Leaving Jessie with Libby, Ella hurried down the corridor, jerking her head towards an examination room to let Kate know she wanted to see her privately.

Swiftly she explained the crisis.

'No one else might get it—but we can't take the risk,' she added. 'Phone Melody West from the preschool and ask her if she could phone all the families with children in Carrie and Jessie's class. We'll start with them, give them the antibiotic that could prevent them getting the wretched disease, but they should all be vaccinated as well.'

Ella paused, marshalling her thoughts.

'And send home any patient who isn't desperately in need of attention. Tell them I'll see them…' When *could* she see them? '…six o'clock tonight.'

'But it's the SES fundraiser tonight,' Kate reminded her, and Ella smiled.

'That'll test just how sick they really are, then,' she said.

'But you're supposed to be going to it.'

Ella shrugged away Kate's protest.

'I'm late to functions so often no one will see it as anything different.'

Kate bustled out to get things organised while Ella found the drug she needed to begin treatment and returned to Jessie and her mother.

'Jessie needs to be in hospital.' She swabbed the little girl's arm and with gentle murmurs of encouragement gave her the needle. 'She's in the initial stages of the disease at the moment, but she needs to be monitored closely. You've two choices,' she said to Libby. 'You can wait for the ambulance to come back to town to take her up to the city, or drive her there yourself. If you decide to do that, I'll give you a note to give the doctor at the Children's Hospital to tell them what I've given her, and phone them to let them know you're coming.'

'We'll take her,' Libby said. 'I don't want to wait.'

'Is Bill available to go with you?'

Libby smiled—a wan effort but better than nothing.

'He'd better be,' she said. 'Actually, he's at cricket with Paul. Oh, my goodness! What about Paul? What if he gets it?'

'I'll give you a script for some antibiotics for him to take. It comes as tablets or raspberry flavoured syrup—which would he take?'

'The syrup every time.'

Ella wrote a script and passed it to Libby.

'I imagine you and Bill would prefer tablets. I want you all to take the antibiotics. I'll phone Jeff at the chemist to tell him you'll be in. He'll have everything waiting for you.'

She walked Libby out to her car and helped her settle Jessie into her car seat.

Frustration with the situation—one ambulance and the nearest hospital two hours away—tightened her muscles as she returned to the storeroom and checked her supplies of vaccine. Jeff Courtney, the pharmacist, would have the rifampicin—she'd ask him to stay open. Do the vaccinations here, then send the families down to Jeff for the antibiotics…

But the vaccine protected against only two groups—did you give the vaccine anyway or wait for the results of Carrie's PCR test? If Carrie had serogroup B then the vaccine was useless.

Expert help, that's what she needed—and fortunately she knew an expert.

She gave a little grimace, aware she hadn't called Rick since they'd broken up, but they'd been good friends—housemates even—for a long time before they'd become—oh, so briefly—lovers, and Rick was the king of experts when it came to epidemics!

She hurried back to her office, lifting the phone receiver and dialling a familiar number.

Please, be home!

A silent prayer answered—no, not answered. It was a woman saying hello.

'Is Rick there? It's…' Not wanting to get Rick into trouble with a new girlfriend, she mumbled her name. Then she added, 'I need to speak to him about precautionary treatment for meningococcal in preschoolers.' There was a brief pause.

'Rick Martin!'

Ella didn't feel a twinge of anything as she heard his voice. But, then, there'd been more affection than love in her feelings for Rick.

'It's Ella, Rick. Sorry to bother you but I've got a problem and I need some advice.'

She explained the situation.

'Two patients isn't a cluster, Ella,' he said, all business immediately, 'but it's a warning the town might be in trouble. Where's the ambulance taking the little girl?'

'City Kids'.'

'I'll get on to someone there and make sure they do the PCR test a.s.a.p. You could have the results in five or six hours, but you need to be aware that these tests can be negative in the acute stages of the disease, though testing later will show up the grouping.'

Silence on the end of the phone told Ella he was thinking, and she was willing to give him all the time he needed. Whatever she did next, it was crucial to get it right—especially with so many young lives at stake.

'Go with the rifampicin,' he said at last. 'The vaccine won't stop kids who are already affected from getting it, but if you can get the antibiotic into everyone who's been in close contact with the affected children, then by Monday at the latest you should know the serogroup and if it's A or C you can start vaccinating.'

Another pause.

'They're trialling a group B vaccine in New Zealand at the moment. If it proves to be group B, maybe we could persuade the powers that be to let us trial it here.'

Ella smiled to herself. She felt no jealousy towards the

woman in Rick's life, but she did feel a little sorry for her. Too often Rick had cancelled plans he'd made with *her* the moment he'd got wind of some new project to attack. She knew within a couple of hours he'd have all the information on the New Zealand trial and be ruining the weekends of Health Department bureaucrats by discussing the possibility of using the vaccine, should it be needed, in Edenvale.

She thanked him and hung up, pleased she had expert advice on how to proceed.

In the meantime, there were other patients to see—as many as she could before the preschoolers started arriving.

Preschoolers!

Brianna!

Her heart prompted her to dash up to the house and check her niece's body for any sign of the disease, but not that long ago she'd showered her and towelled her dry—and not seen a spot!

But for the first time since Brianna had come into her life, she found herself facing the dilemma of what came first— family or patients.

Patients won out—just—and she'd seen three more before Nash reappeared in the surgery.

'OK, what's the plan?' he asked, joining her in the now empty waiting room.

She frowned at him, not understanding the question.

'For the children who've been in close contact with Carrie? You're going to start a vaccination programme surely.'

'I'm going to examine as many of them as I can today and prescribe antibiotics. By this evening I should have a sero-group type—if I'm lucky. Then I can think about vaccination.'

Nash frowned suspiciously at her.

'You've made this decision yourself? No consultation with someone who might just happen to know a little more about meningococcal outbreaks than you do?'

It would be so easy to tell him she *had* consulted someone, but his attitude infuriated her so she lifted her chin, glared into the silvery eyes and said, 'And just what business is it of yours? You come bowling down here to visit your mother for the first time in months and, OK, it was a help to have a second opinion on Carrie, but then you sit there, counting my patients, totting up how much I must be making in an hour, disturbing me by just being there, and now you've got the hide to be telling me what I should and shouldn't be doing.'

His frown became more ferocious—beating her glare hands down.

'You're forgetting just one thing!' he stormed. 'This is my town and I care about the people in it!'

'Care about the people in it, or are you more worried an incompetent GP might run your mother's practice into the ground and reduce its value? You ignore your mother for months, then suddenly she mentions selling out and you can't get here quickly enough. Are you sure it isn't money and not people you're thinking of?'

She saw a smear of heat redden his strong cheekbones and knew she'd pushed too far, but her nerves were in tatters and her mind too busy with all the other worries to censor her words.

'I care about the people,' he said, savagely emphasising each word. 'The people in this town who've already suffered enough!'

He didn't add 'at the hands of a Marsden' but he didn't need to. It was there—implicit in his voice as well as in the words. Ella felt all her blood draining to her feet. Determined not to let him beat her, she summoned every ounce of will-power she possessed, lifted her chin, straightened her shoulders and met his furious gaze.

'Fine way you have of showing it!' she snapped, then turned away. Cars pulling into the car park told her the first of the preschoolers, summoned by Melody West, had arrived.

Nash contemplated following her into her office and continuing the argument, but judging from the cars pulling up outside she'd soon be inundated by small patients.

They'd all have to be examined.

Should he offer to help?

Why the hell should he after the way she'd spoken to him?

But he hadn't pulled any punches either, and as his anger cooled he realised he *had* to help. That was what being a doctor was all about.

'Hi, stranger!'

Bob Carruthers, his best mate all through school, was carrying two howling children in his arms.

'Staying for the SES fundraiser tonight? I'd have a better chance of catching up with you at that than while I'm hauling these brats to the doctor's.'

Then Bob frowned, shushed his children, and stepped closer.

'It's dangerous, isn't it, this meningococcal thing?'

Nash saw the worry in his old friend's eyes and wondered just how badly *his* gut would twist if his child or children were in this situation.

'Antibiotics will stave it off, and when we know what variant of the disease we're dealing with we can vaccinate. But, yes, it's a nasty thing and hopefully all children will eventually be immunised against it.'

Other worried-looking parents were coming in, and Nash crossed to the reception desk.

'Is there a second room I can use?' he asked, knowing his father had often employed a locum during the summer holidays.

Kate eyed him doubtfully.

'I'd have to check with Ella.'

'No, I'll check with her,' Nash said, seeing a mother and child come out of Ella's office. 'I'll whip in there before she calls the next patient.'

She was tapping information into a computer, a pair of black-rimmed glasses perched on her nose—looking for all the world like a child playing 'grown-ups'.

The last remnants of his anger died.

'I can help,' he said, blurting out the words because seeing her like that had jolted something inside him. She'd worn glasses when she'd studied, back when she'd asked him if he'd coach her in maths, offering to pay him with the money she made working weekends at the supermarket. He'd taken them off before he'd kissed her that first time…

Ella glanced up and he could see she was remembering his angry accusations and not a kiss from the past. Her eyes were wary, but eventually she smiled and though it was an 'I suppose you're better than no one' kind of smile, Nash found himself smiling back.

'Thanks,' she said, the smile replaced by a concerned frown. 'I don't know if you heard but I've found a second case from the same preschool class. The children coming in now are all in that class. I'm examining the kids for a rash, explaining the situation to the parents, telling them I might want to vaccinate the children as well and getting their written permission to do that. I'm also handing out an information leaflet that tells them what to look for and insisting they contact me if they are at all worried.'

She paused, studying him as if trying to work out if she should tell him more. Given her opinion of him as an uncaring money-grubber, he wondered if she would.

But something she'd seen in that scrutiny must have reassured her for she continued her explanation.

'I thought if I have to vaccinate I'd do it at the preschool Monday morning, which is why I'm getting the parents to sign permission forms now. In a number of the families both parents work, so coming back to the surgery on Monday could be disruptive.'

'So I examine them, explain and give them a leaflet and a script for the antibiotic—then get written authority to vaccinate if it proves necessary?'

Ella nodded, aware of the difference it would make, having a second doctor to help check the children. If they could pick up a symptom at a very early stage, the child would have a much better chance of complete recovery. That alone made her sorry she'd yelled at him earlier!

'I really appreciate this, Nash,' she said. 'The room across the corridor is all set up as a second consulting room—I've been looking for another locum to help out over the holidays.'

He turned away, and as he went out the door Ella rested her head on her hands for a few moments.

What was it with Nash that his presence, even when he was offering her help, had her as tense as fencing wire?

Was it just her fear that he could stop her buying the practice? Or something more?

And what was it with her that her heart still misbehaved when she looked at the man?

'All done?'

Two hours had passed, and Ella looked up wearily from the computer screen to see Nash standing in the doorway.

'All done,' she echoed, her voice scratchy with tiredness, then the fear she'd felt earlier gripped her heart.

Fear and, worse, guilt that she'd, if only temporarily, forgotten.

'Brianna!' she said. 'I have to check Brianna.'

A look of what might have been compassion crossed Nash's face.

'You've done enough for today. I'll check her for you,' he offered, then he held up his hand as if to ward off an expected argument. 'I worked A and E at various children's hospitals in the UK when I was working over there. I'll be extremely thorough.'

Ella nodded. She'd be thorough herself, but it was far better to have someone impartial examine Brianna.

She nodded, hoping she wasn't revealing the stomach-clutching, bowel-knotting, heart-faltering fear she felt for the little girl.

'I'll pop up to the house and get her. I've been marking off the ones we've seen. There are twenty-four children in Jessie and Carrie's class and, not counting Brianna, all but four have been in. Melody, the preschool teacher, is still trying to track down those four.'

She looked at Nash.

'I'm wondering if I should spread the checks further, but at the same time I don't want to panic the whole population of Edenvale.'

'Go and get Brianna,' Nash told her, his voice so gentle it brought a lump of emotion to Ella's throat.

She swallowed hard and reminded herself he was the enemy. Only Nash could stop his mother selling, so getting emotional over gently spoken words was *not a good thing*!

'Yes,' she said, and walked out, stopping on the way to tell Kate to pack up and go home.

'And don't come back tonight,' she added as she walked through the door. 'With the fundraiser on, most of the patients will cure themselves. I can manage on my own.'

Not that Kate would take any notice. Though she only worked part time, she fussed over Ella like a mother hen. Ella hoped Kate wouldn't go into her consulting room for something before she departed and find the undrunk glass of milk and uneaten plate of sandwiches she'd brought in for Ella hours earlier.

There'd hardly been time to breathe, let alone eat!

Neither Brianna nor Mrs Carter were at the house, but the joyous noises coming from the garden behind the cottage told Ella the children must be there.

And as she walked towards the special space Sarah had created, not only for Brianna but for all the children of Edenvale, her anxiety and tension lifted, so by the time she entered the sweet-scented, flowering magic of the fairy garden, her smile was natural, not forced.

Though Karen didn't seem to find the delightful garden as uplifting. She must have heard Ella's footsteps and had turned, no doubt expecting Nash. Her face fell, and her impatient look was replaced by one of anger.

'How you could even think of selling the practice to someone so incompetent that Nash has had to spend all his visit down at the surgery helping out, I don't know.'

The words had obviously been directed at Sarah, who was

threading daisies on a chain to crown Brianna, but the angry look accompanying them was aimed straight at Ella.

'Any more cases?' Sarah asked, setting the crown on Brianna's head and promising Pete she'd do one for him next.

'Just the two so far,' Ella told her. 'There are four we haven't seen…' Long pause! 'And Brianna,' she added in a strangled voice.

'I think you'll find she's fine,' Sarah said, then she looked anxiously at Ella. 'Should *you* be examining her?'

'I'd have to do it if Nash wasn't here,' Ella reminded her, 'but, no, I won't. He'll check her out.'

She turned to the child and took her hand.

'Come on, poppet. Carrie and Jessie from your preschool class are sick, and Nash, who's another doctor, wants to take a look at you and make sure you're not getting the same thing.'

'Is it measles?' asked Brianna, whose favourite book was about a child with measles.

'It's like measles,' Ella told her.

Only far more deadly, she added in her head, fear again rising because being a doctor didn't mean she could save this precious child if she'd already contracted the terrible disease. She told herself to calm down. They'd picked up Carrie's symptoms early, but that didn't stop her peering at Brianna's face—willing there not to be any tell-tale spots.

She couldn't see any yet, but only time could tell.

Nash sensed Ella's reluctance as they entered the room he'd been using, though if anyone should feel awkward it was him. This was, after all, her surgery—though he'd made the mistake of forgetting that once already today.

'You already know there's no rash, and if she's not been feeling unwell, there's nothing to worry about,' he said quietly, and tormented hazel eyes slanted his way.

'I've been telling myself that all the way down the drive,' she admitted. 'But it doesn't seem to work.'

Nash looked at the beautiful child standing so trustingly between them, a crown of daisies threaded through her bright curly hair. He didn't think it would work for him either if Brianna had been his child...

'Come on, let's take a look at you, Miss Brianna,' he said, lifting her onto the table where she sat and smiled at him, sandalled feet and brown legs swinging.

'At school you call the teachers Miss,' she told him. 'I'll be going to school soon.'

'Not very soon, poppet,' Ella said. 'Pete goes next year but you and Carrie have to wait another year.'

'I should go with Pete,' Brianna said, while Nash showed Ella the readout on the thermometer—normal. 'He's my best friend and best friends should always be together.'

Nash knew he couldn't possibly remember what Meg and Ella had been like at Brianna's age—he probably hadn't known them at all until they'd gone to school—but he did remember the pair's insistence that they were best friends and best friends should always be together. It had been impossible to get Ella to go out with him on a date unless he'd found a friend to take Meg. Not that finding an obliging friend had been difficult. The girls had had a reputation for being wild, a reputation Nash—and his friends—had soon found totally ill-founded.

Now remembered guilt swamped the little bit of warmth remembered kisses had provided earlier. He'd done nothing to stop that rumour spreading...

Though Russell had.

Russell, who'd fallen so hard for Meg he'd fought a lout who'd called her a tart, yet Russell still hadn't won her heart...

'Are you OK?'

He turned to find Ella eyeing him anxiously.

'Just thinking,' he said lamely, turning his attention back to the child he was examining.

'There's no temp and no sign of a rash, so let's go with

the antibiotic and wait until we know a serogroup,' he said, lifting Brianna down off the couch. 'Is the chemist still open?'

Guilt must be catching—it was certainly evident on Ella's face.

'Oh, poor Jeff,' she said. 'I should have phoned him earlier and told him we'd finished with the preschoolers. I've enough doses here for Brianna, and the other four if Melody finds them.'

'Jeff Courtney? Did he take over the shop from his father?'

'His father still runs it—can you imagine Mr Courtney handing over control of anything?—but he takes the weekend off these days.' She lifted the receiver and pressed a number on the keypad. 'Jeff? Ella. I've done all but four and have enough rifampicin here for them so there's no need for you to stay longer. Thanks so much for helping out.'

A pause, then Nash would have sworn Ella blushed before saying, 'I've got patients I put off from this morning to see at six so I don't know what time I'll be there, but I'll try to make it.'

She hung up quickly and bent over Brianna.

Definitely blushing.

'Don't tell me you're seeing something of Jeff Courtney,' Nash thought—or thought he thought, but the words must have sneaked out without him knowing, for a different flush now lit Ella's cheeks.

'And just what business is it of yours? Are you so keen to rid *your* town of Marsdens you're going to tell me who I can and can't see?'

'Whom! It should be whom!' he said helpfully, then ducked because he'd stirred her up so much he was sure she'd throw something.

She restrained herself—maybe because she didn't have anything in her hand to throw—and turned to Brianna.

'Come on, Brianna,' Ella said with immense dignity. 'I'll get you some medicine from the storeroom that will stop you getting what Carrie's got, then we'll go home and you can have a sleep before the party.'

Nash watched them walk out, not thinking of Ella now—well, not entirely—but of the SES fundraiser. Until she'd told Brianna she'd need a sleep, he'd forgotten what a huge annual event it was in Edenvale. Although its primary aim was to raise money for new equipment and to help with the running costs of the local State Emergency Service, a volunteer organization, it was also the main event of the town's holiday season. When he was growing up, it had been like a signal that Christmas was nearly here, and the excitement among the children had always been enormous.

Mainly, he realised now, because it was one of the few evening events to which children were specifically invited. The SES was a family affair, sons and daughters following their parents into the emergency service. It heralded the first appearance in town of Santa Claus, though he came not in a sleigh drawn by reindeer but riding atop the fire truck, siren wailing, Santa waving and throwing handfuls of sweets to the children who ran beside the truck.

His mother had always told him and Russell not to grab too many, pointing out there were poor children in the town who didn't have money to buy sweets. Russell might have listened—he'd always been a softie—but Nash remembered grabbing as many as he could, though he'd shared them with his mates later...

Would Brianna be there to welcome Santa and run beside the fire engine if Ella was working?

He could offer to work in her place...

Only then *he'd* miss the party...

'You're not going to the party,' he reminded himself, muttering the words out loud so he could be certain he understood them. 'You're going back to the city and having dinner with some friends of Karen's.'

Surely he wasn't feeling regret that he'd be sipping a decent Riesling and discussing share portfolios instead of standing around a huge barbeque pit with the smell of roast lamb and crisp pork crackling rising in the air, discussing the likelihood of Australia beating India in the upcoming cricket test series.

Or the price of milk! According to his mother, that was the local concern at the moment. Edenvale had always been the centre of a rich dairy industry but now the price of milk was very low and developers were offering big money for property, so families who'd farmed for years were wondering what to do for the best, the men especially not at all sure that money could provide them with a life they'd enjoy when all they'd known all their lives had been farming...

CHAPTER THREE

'ARE you thinking deep and meaningful thoughts that you're still standing where I left you minutes ago?' Ella asked.

'I was thinking about the price of milk.' He spoke grumpily, sorry she'd caught him staring into space and distracted yet again by his reaction to her presence—linked, he had no doubt, to some hangover from the past.

'Sarah's been talking to you.' Ella led the way to the door, waited until he'd walked out then locked it.

Brianna ran on ahead up the drive, and Ella continued. 'Sarah's worried that people who've worked all their lives won't know what to do with themselves if they sell up and have enough money to retire.'

He grasped at the topic as a drowning man might grasp a lifeline. Far better to talk retirement than consider why Ella was having this strange effect on him.

'But business people, public servants, a lot of folk are retiring younger,' he pointed out.

'Those people, squirrelling away their superannuation so they have financial security later, have planned for their retirement and developed interests to carry on when they stop work. Farmers aren't into retirement planning, and I doubt many have superannuation. They've always thought they'd go on for ever, staying on at the farm even when their sons or daughters take over the running of it.'

Ella walked beside him, glad to have a relatively harmless subject to discuss. Although discussing the security of dairy farmers was skirting dangerously close to other things she didn't want to think about.

Not right now.

'Have the farmers who've sold to developers stayed in the town?'

Another easy question.

'I know two who have, but they're the only ones I know who've sold.'

She was managing—just—to keep up her end of the conversation, but Nash's presence was disturbing her, and not only, she was honest enough to admit, because she was worried he'd persuade Sarah not to sell the practice.

Surely the teenage crush she'd had on him hadn't lingered on, resurfacing now as an attraction towards the man. Making its presence felt in an inner disquiet every time she looked at him.

Not that she had to look at him. This new Nash seemed imprinted on her mind.

Dark hair cut ruthlessly short, showing a few flecks of grey at the temples. Tanned skin, beard shadow and a strong straight nose between those silvery eyes. She could even see the way one eye closed slightly when he half smiled, tilting up one side of his very kissable lips and causing smile wrinkles on that side of his face.

Smile wrinkles!

Kissable lips!

What *was* this stuff?

'Travel.'

'I'm sorry, I wasn't listening.'

They were at the house and Brianna had ducked around the back, no doubt keen to return to Sarah's garden. But both children should have a rest before tonight, so Ella would follow her and collect Pete and bring them both back to the house.

'You're still not listening.'

She looked up at Nash—at the face she'd been trying not to notice—and her heart skipped a beat. That damn crush wasn't crushed at all. Though how she could feel like this about a man who was aiming to ruin all her plans, she didn't know!

'I'm sorry. I was thinking ahead. I want Pete to have a rest, but that's a bit like asking a puppy not to chew shoes. I'm reasonably sure he's not hyperactive, but he does have boundless energy. If he won't lie on a bed and read a book, I'll sit him down in front of a video. Television as a pacifier.'

Realising she was rattling on because of that skipped heartbeat, she offered an apologetic smile then hurried after Brianna.

'Oh, it's you again,' Karen greeted her. 'Where's Nash?'

'He's right behind me,' Ella told her, but when she turned, he wasn't.

Oh, well, Nash McLaren was a big boy now—he could look after himself. Thanking Sarah for minding Pete, she rounded up both children, took them by the hand and led them back to the house.

'Time for a rest,' she informed them both. Brianna went off quite happily to her room, Harry, her special dog, tagging along behind her. And for once Pete didn't argue, climbing up onto Ella's bed without the slightest protest. Though as she handed him a picture book about fire engines, his dark eyes looked up at her and his voice quivered as he asked, 'Will Carrie be all right?'

Ella gathered him in her arms and hugged him tight.

'She might be sick for a little while, but the doctors will do all they can to make her better,' she assured him, praying in her heart the words wouldn't prove to be a lie. 'You look at the pictures while I check on Brianna, then I'll come back and read the book to you.'

Nash was standing just outside the bedroom door. He looked embarrassed and uncomfortable but not half as embarrassed and uncomfortable as Ella felt. That morning's argument was forgotten and now *she* was in the wrong.

Or felt she was.

'This must seem terrible to you—as if I've kicked Sarah out of her house. Look, I have to check on Brianna, then I'll try to explain…'

Only she'd promised to read to Pete…

'I'll read to Pete,' Nash offered, and she could only stare at him.

'Go on,' he said, smiling at her confusion. 'Settle Brianna. We can talk later.'

Brianna was already asleep, a raggedy bear clutched against her chest. Ella stood for a moment looking at her, thinking how much Bear meant to the little girl. He represented security, and over the last five months it had gradually dawned on Ella that *her* security—her Bear—was the town of Edenvale.

Now Nash was here, following her around at work, wandering around the house—more his house than hers...

Pain seized her lungs, leaving her breathless with panic.

Sarah had assured Ella that Nash didn't want the house or the practice, but now a really scary thought had her struggling for breath again. He might not want it for himself but how far would he go to prevent a Marsden getting it?

Like most of the town, he'd decided her father had been a liar and a cheat, rather than a man who lost a lot of the locals' money through drunken incompetence, and on top of that there was Russell—his bright, funny, brilliant and mercurial younger brother.

That he blamed Meg for Russell's death Ella had no doubt, but hearts couldn't fall in love to order, and Meg had never loved Russ—not the way he'd wanted her to...

Nash came out of the room where Pete was resting while she stood there, transfixed by her thoughts.

'You were going to explain,' he said, his eyes seeming more blue than grey in the shadowed light of the hall.

Ella shook her head.

'I was, but I've already taken up too much of your time. You came down to spend the day with your mother, and she's barely seen you.'

She paused, curbing an unexpected renewal of the anger she'd harboured against him for the way he'd been neglecting his mother.

'I'm really grateful you *were* here,' she added, nice words to hide that anger, 'but Sarah's missing out on your company.'

'Sarah will see plenty of me,' he said, and she could swear he was deliberately provoking her. 'I've decided to stay the night. Catch up with some old friends at the fundraiser.'

Ha! That got her. Nash watched the frown quiver between her eyebrows before she smiled—falsely—and said with equally false enthusiasm, 'How nice for Sarah!'

'That's actually why I came into the house—uninvited.' He was on a roll now, relishing her discomfort, telling himself she deserved it, though one last remaining shred of decency told him he was being petty. 'To see if some of the things I left here were still in my room—or did you shift me down to the cottage as well?'

Now, don't go soft because she looks a trifle pale, he warned himself, but the paleness didn't last long enough for him to worry—replaced by a fiery red that could only signal anger.

'I haven't touched a thing on that side of the house.' A force-ten glare accompanied the words. 'Sarah might have shifted your things, though it's so long since you've been down you've probably outgrown them, like you've outgrown this town for all your talk earlier. And moving in here wasn't my idea—it was Sarah's. She said the house was too big for her and she missed the noise that had filled it when you and Russell and your father lived here.'

Missed Russell, who'd lived with her a lot of the time, the bit of decency remaining in Nash's heart admitted. But not out loud. Not when Ella had done nothing more than pause for breath before continuing her tirade.

'In practical terms, I was going to get a live-in nanny so there'd always be someone close by for Brianna, but Sarah pointed out that if I lived here, then Mrs Carter could do that job. I pay Mrs Carter all her wages, even though she still does a day's cleaning down at the cottage for your mother, and I pay your mother rent for the house as well. Satisfied?'

Ella shook her head to try to clear the anger, but it

still simmered beneath her skin so strongly it was like a prickly rash.

Prickly enough to prompt her to attack again.

'And maybe if you'd come home more often—brought friends to fill the house occasionally—your mother mightn't have felt so lonely, and may not have wanted to move.'

Nash said nothing—not in his own defence, or even about her explanation. He just looked at her so intently Ella's anger died away and embarrassment now crept in to replace it.

'I've got things to do,' she said, and turned away, then remembered where this conversation had started. 'Feel free to go and check your old room.'

Nash watched her walk away, not back to the bedrooms but towards the kitchen. And thinking of the kitchen reminded him he'd missed lunch. No doubt Ella had as well. Was she making a sandwich? Could he join her there? Would she yell at him again?

He was surprised to find that option didn't bother him. His conscience had told him most of the things she'd said about him were true. In fact, his conscience had been far harsher.

But if she was renting the house, why wasn't she living in the other side? Using his mother's old bedroom instead of the small one where Pete was resting?

Walking through the doorway of that room had been enough to tell Nash it was Ella's—the scent in the air indefinable but definitely female. But the narrow single bed was neatly made, the room as tidy as a nun's cell, and with about as much character.

Was it possible Ella was embarrassed about living in the house?

A Marsden embarrassed?

Hardly likely!

Or did she not want to settle in—to make the place home-like—in case the sale fell through and she had to move on when her time was up?

He shook his head, aware he didn't know her well enough to even begin to guess, and went towards his old bedroom—

the one he'd shared with Russell. It was twice the size of the one Ella was using, and though all traces of their occupation had been removed—no doubt by his mother—its air was still redolent of his youth. He sank down on the double bed that had replaced the two singles of their childhood and looked around at familiar walls and bookshelves and the window that opened towards the sea.

A window the pair of them had climbed out of so often—to meet up with Bob, and Josh Mills, and whoever else had been in the 'gang' at the time, Russell always tagging along though he had been two years younger. Their midnight pursuits had been innocent enough, creeping into the lava tubes and scaring themselves silly when bats had flown about in protest, or going swimming in the surf, a practice forbidden by their parents who'd believed sharks ate more people at night than they did in the daytime.

And in their teenage years, throwing small stones at the bedroom windows of girls they'd fancied, and holding whispered conversations with their Juliets!

'Sarah will have saved something for you, but I've made some sandwiches and a pot of coffee if you want some sustenance while you brood.'

Ella stood in the doorway, framed by the jamb.

'Was it always you who came to the window those nights?' he asked her, swept along on the tide of remembrance. 'Or did you sometimes swap around with Meg?'

Ella hesitated a moment, then she must have caught his train of thought for she smiled—reluctantly.

'We swapped at school from time to time,' she admitted, 'to fool the teachers, and occasionally when we were dating, but I don't think we ever did with you.

'It wasn't very nice of us, was it?' she added, her face and voice grave. 'But life wasn't very nice for us at the time, and we took whatever fun we could.'

She turned away, leaving Nash to realise that he'd never once considered the Marsden twins' life from their side. Their mother had left when they'd been entering their teenage years, deserting her husband and children for an itinerant surfer ten years her junior. Their father, who'd managed the co-op, had begun drinking—or maybe he'd always been a drinker, and just did it more openly, and in more volume after his wife departed. Then things had gone bad at the co-op and more than half the families in town, the McLarens included, had lost money.

The town had been quick to point a finger—labelling Tom Marsden a cheat as well as a drunkard.

Labelling the girls wild…

Oh, for heaven's sake, don't start feeling sorry for her!

He heaved himself off the bed and followed her to the kitchen. He'd walk straight through it and down to the cottage. His mother *would* have saved some lunch for him, Karen would be spitting chips, and that was *before* he told her they were staying the night.

'No! No way! Stay if you think that woman can't handle a little outbreak of meningococcal on her own, but don't expect me to miss the Beavises' party. I'll take your car back to the city. You can hire a car to drive back tomorrow. That's if this excuse for a town runs to hire cars.'

His mind boggled over the 'little outbreak of meningococcal'. Karen was a doctor and would know the seriousness of the disease. To downplay it in such a way made him cringe on her behalf—*and* wonder if all the weekends he'd worked lately had really been because the department had been short of staff! Or had it been an avoidance tactic…?

Maybe he should have told her the real reason he wanted to stay—to stand around the barbeque pit and feel the familiarity of home. Would she stay with him? He knew the answer to that one. She'd give him a horrified look and possibly suggest he have a psychiatric assessment. Though the thought of her standing around the barbeque pit with a can of beer in her hand made it difficult to bite back a smile.

He stuck with meningococcal.

'I'm sorry, but I feel obliged. A lot of the people I saw

earlier—the parents of the kids who could be affected—are old friends. I'd be letting them down if I left.'

It was prime rubbish—Ella had shown herself more than capable—but Karen seemed slightly appeased by it, leaning forward to kiss his cheek.

'You're too kind for your own good. I'm always telling you that. It's why you take on all the extra shifts at work and rarely have a weekend off. I was hoping this holiday might be different.'

She stepped back and he knew the sentimental moment had passed.

'But you will be back tomorrow in time for the opening of Charlie's art exhibition.' A statement, not a question. 'Everyone who's anyone will be there, and you've known him longer than most people, so you're kind of a guest of honour.'

Nash hid a sigh. It wasn't Charlie's fault his art had taken off and his paintings were selling for five-figure sums, which meant the opening of one of his exhibitions had gone from cask wine accompanied by stale biscuits and dry cheese to champagne and catered canapé affairs. Nash had preferred the cask-wine days, while for Karen, his friendship with Charlie, begun when they'd shared a house with other students while they'd been at university, was an entrée into the highest level of the social elite.

'I'll try,' he said to Karen, but she hadn't waited for an answer. Taking his assent for granted, she was already saying goodbye to his mother. 'If I'm going back on my own, I might as well go now,' she was saying. 'That way you can have him all to yourself.'

Sarah didn't argue—didn't even make a polite 'Oh, do stay' protest. Maybe undiluted Karen for a few hours had worn down even his mother's well-known patience.

'Why are you really staying?' Sarah asked him when he returned from seeing Karen off.

'Because Ella needs help,' Nash told her.

His mother's response—a dry 'Really?'—confirmed his own inner belief that with only four more children to see Ella didn't need help at all. Even if she opted to do a mass vaccination on Monday she'd have the surgery nurses to help her.

The truth was he didn't know why he was staying. It was partly to do with seeing Bob, and partly to do with sitting in his bedroom, thinking about Russell. It was maybe even to do with seeing Ella again after all this time and very little, he realised with a renewed pang of conscience, to do with spending more time with his mother.

She was talking about the garden, leading him to the kitchen where she delved into the fridge and came out with a salad on a plate, plastic-wrap-covered as his father's meals so often had been.

'I saw a fairy garden on a television show—someone made one at a children's hospital—and I thought to myself, I could do that. Mrs Carter helped, and Ella, and Brianna. Brianna is actually the best help as she just does as she's told, while the others offer suggestions that don't always fit with my plan.'

Nash listened as he ate, thinking how young his mother sounded, seeing again how freely she moved.

'You'd given up gardening,' he reminded her, and she beamed at him.

'Oh, that was because my arthritis was so bad. I'd get down and not be able to get up again. But Ella had heard of this antibiotic treatment for rheumatoid arthritis—and believed it worked for what I had, which was psoriatic arthritis. Anyway, she found out all about it, asked me if I'd like to be a guinea pig—and here I am.'

She held her arms wide as if to show she could move freely, then offered her hands.

'Of course, the old swellings haven't gone down because the joints were already damaged, but I don't get that painful red swelling in my fingers and toes any more. My knees still trouble me, but Ella says if the tablets continue to work it might be worth having knee replacements and starting afresh with them.'

'Why doesn't she live in our side of the house?'

It probably wasn't the question his mother was expecting—or the one he should have asked. He'd kind of ignored the garden conversation but shouldn't he have shown at least a modicum of interest in his mother's health?

'I did urge her to.' His mother seemed unfazed by his lack of interest in her condition. 'Maybe it's because Mrs Carter is on the other side in the wing your grandfather built for his sister and her children. Ella might have decided it's better to be close to Mrs Carter so she'll hear Brianna if she's called out, although she uses a baby monitor and just puts the receiver outside Mrs Carter's room if she does go out at night, and that would work equally well from the other side of the house.'

Sarah stared out the window for a moment, then added, 'She's a very private person, Ella. And self-effacing somehow. As if she feels that if the town doesn't notice she's here, she might be able to stay.'

'Why wouldn't she be able to stay?' Nash demanded, and his mother gave him a long look.

'*You* know how the town treated those girls after their father lost all that money for the co-op! It wasn't long after it happened that your father died and my excuse was I was grieving for him,' she said quietly, 'but that doesn't stop me feeling guilty now I think back on it. They were ostracised not for themselves but because of who their father was. Then Tom Marsden drank himself to death and they had no one. Of course she'd feel uncertain about her welcome.'

Nash pushed his half-eaten lunch away, his mind telling him he should have gone back to the city with Karen, while a far too vivid picture of the past flickered in his head.

He'd broken up with Ella before her father had died, but Russell had still doggedly pursued an unresponsive Meg. Russell had suggested they go and see the girls—offer condolences and ask if there was anything they could do—but Nash had refused, mainly because of guilt at how he'd treated Ella…

'Russell asked if they could come and live here until they finished school. Did you know that?'

'Good grief, Mum! He asked you that? When? Three months after Dad died, when it was likely that the stress from losing all that money had contributed to his heart attack? And now you're anxious to sell to Ella, of all people! Is it a guilt trip? Some kind of recompense because, when you were grieving the loss of my father, you didn't take time out to look after the Marsden twins? And aren't you forgetting one other small thing? OK, so Dad might have been heading for a heart attack anyway, but Russell certainly died because of Meg!'

'No, Nash, that's wrong and you know it. Russell was sick, and if it hadn't been Meg's last rejection of him, it would have been something else that triggered his final fight with depression. You can't blame Meg—she couldn't help not loving him.'

She paused, fixing him with a 'stern-mother' look.

'And you can't blame Ella. Ella's a fine doctor,' his mother said.

'But why would she come back here, when she must have known what she'd be up against?'

'I don't know,' his mother said, and though they were simple words he heard his own doubt in them. His mother might defend Ella, but she, too, was concerned about what had prompted a Marsden to return to Edenvale.

To a place where her name was hated and reviled...

Sarah walked away before he could ask more questions, out into the garden he hadn't even looked at, although he'd heard the pride and satisfaction in her voice when she'd talked about it.

So much for staying in Edenvale to spend more time with his mother!

The anger he'd felt earlier when he'd first seen Ella had returned, and while he'd like to think it was because of the curse the Marsdens seem to carry for his family, if he was honest with himself, it was probably more to do with guilt—

guilt at how he'd treated Ella back when they'd been teenagers.

Guilt that he hadn't had enough compassion to accompany Russell on that visit of condolence…

Was *that* why Ella had come back? To make the whole damn town feel guilty?

He tipped what was left of his lunch into the bin, washed his plate and dried it, then followed his mother into the garden.

Ella sat at the kitchen table, staring at the cheese sandwich she'd made for herself, telling herself she had to eat. But it was impossible to eat with her mind going round and round in circles—Carrie, Nash, vaccinations, Nash, Jessie, Nash, meningococcal, Nash—while her stomach churned in sympathy with the mental confusion.

One thing at a time, Ella told herself. Both Carrie and Jessie would be in hospital by now, getting the very best of treatment so they had the best possible chance of a complete recovery. There was no point in worrying about the long-term effects meningococcal could have on them if the disease took hold—scarring, deafness, loss of limbs—so she shut her mind to it, telling herself to think positively.

Or if positive was impossible, think practical!

The meningococcal outbreak, if it was an outbreak, was contained as much as it could be at present. As soon as Melody tracked down the other four children, the close preschool contacts would be covered. Pete was OK, and his parents would be treated with rifampicin at the hospital.

So with those worries sorted, she was left with Nash…

Nash didn't matter.

Easy to say, harder to believe.

Nash was not at all happy about Sarah selling the practice to a Marsden. He hadn't exactly said as much—not to Ella— but he'd made it patently obvious, disapproval straightening his broad shoulders and lifting his strong chin to an arrogant level when he'd first recognised her that morning.

So, was that all that was bothering her about Nash?

Of course it was!

Liar.

She stood up, tipped the cheese sandwich into the bin and went to check on Pete, who, blessedly, was asleep with the fire-engine book still clutched in his hands.

So she'd had a crush on Nash.

All teenager girls had a crush on *someone*! It was practically obligatory.

And he'd been kind, helping her with her maths and refusing to take payment.

Had he done it not from kindness but to get to know her better? She had no idea, remembering still the shock she'd felt the day he'd taken off her glasses and kissed her on the lips.

Her first kiss!

Not that Nash would have known that—or believed it if she'd told him. The Marsden twins had been labelled wild, and it was easier to believe rumour than truth.

Their first few dates—with Meg and whatever friend Nash had produced to accompany her—had been sedate enough, although their goodnight kisses had grown increasingly fervent. But then, on the beach one moonlit night, he'd gone too far and she'd told him so, breaking out of his embrace, angry and embarrassed. Hot with an inner hunger she hadn't understood, she'd fled the beach, running all the way home to a sister who'd known no more than she had about what went on between men and women, and a father who'd no longer cared about his daughters.

Ella shook away the memories, though not before a smirking Lisa Warren had appeared on the edge of them.

'And a good thing you did, Lisa!' Ella muttered. Remembering how Nash had dumped her for the netball queen should put an end to any nonsense about hangovers from the past as far as Nash McLaren was concerned.

Meg had said all along he'd been only after one thing—why else would he have lowered himself to go out with a

Marsden? Believing the rumours, he'd have expected Ella to fall into his arms, and from there into the back seat of his beat-up old car...

Oh, Meg!

Nash walked through the door, then hesitated.

'I should have knocked.'

Ella shook her head.

'It's still your home,' she said. 'I'm the interloper.'

'That's what I came to say. You're not, and I had no right to make you feel that way, just walking in earlier. Going into my old bedroom. I'm sorry.'

Ella stared at him, wary and confused. Just where was this apology going? Had he made it just to make her feel bad?

'I wanted to ask you about Mum,' he continued, pulling out a chair and turning it so he could sit astride and rest his arms on the back of it. 'She said something about a trial with antibiotics and, having seen her working in the garden, it's like a miracle. Can you tell me more?'

Ella propped herself against the sink, and told herself this was a normal colleague-to-colleague conversation.

She could handle it.

Especially now, with her memories as armour...

'I read about a trial protocol when I had another patient with bad rheumatoid arthritis, where tetracycline drugs were used to treat the disease. The study suggested the derivative minocycline, orally, but only three times a week so there's a break in the presence of it in the body. It's not well tolerated and has to be taken on an empty stomach and the patient monitored closely for side effects, but thankfully your mother's been free of them, and it seems to be working, although the original trial did suggest using it on patients in the early stages of the disease.'

'Tetracycline? It's been around for so long, I guess no one thought to try it on arthritic patients.'

'It's still not classified as a treatment,' Ella told him, keeping the conversation going, although she had a feeling this wasn't what Nash had come about.

Had it simply been to apologise, and this talk of his mother's drugs was making the apology less of a big deal?

Ella didn't think so.

'Why did you come back here, Ella?'

Uh-oh! Sometimes being right wasn't all that great!

She was watching him so warily Nash wondered if she'd answer—and if she did, would she tell the truth? Then she sighed and shrugged her shoulders, drawing his attention to her full breasts—features he'd been trying to put out of his mind since seeing them earlier in the wet T-shirt.

'We had a wonderful childhood, Meg and I. Oh, it went bad later, but no one could take away the freedom and joy of growing up in Edenvale. The beach, the caves, the farmland and hills—it was all perfect.'

She hesitated, still watching him—perhaps daring him to scoff.

'I wanted that for Brianna,' she added. 'Meg wanted it, too. She left a letter, not that she expected to die...'

Nash heard the break in her voice and longed to comfort her, but he had his own pain to deal with where Meg was concerned—the pain of Russell's death.

'In the letter she talked about *our* childhood and about growing up in a small town where the pace of life is slower than in the city and people know and watch out for each other. Then I saw your mother's ad and I thought it was meant to be. The fact that the job was for a locum meant I could try it out—see if it would be as good as I expected it to be. See if I could make it work—juggling work and a child.'

She hesitated then added, 'See if the town would accept me!'

OK, that was all believable—a little sentimental perhaps, but women got that way at times.

So why didn't he believe it?

Or believe those weren't the only reasons she'd returned?

Because she hadn't met his eyes as she'd explained, studying instead the table, and at times the dishcloth she held in her hands? And a flush of pink now tinged her cheeks. The Ella he'd known when he'd been growing up had found it difficult to lie, blushing as she'd told even the most innocent of tales.

He tucked his suspicion away to be examined later.

'It must have worked out, that you want to buy the place,' Nash suggested, and Ella nodded.

'More than I could ever have guessed,' she said softly. 'Brianna has blossomed, though that's as much due to the love she gets from Sarah and Mrs Carter as from the fresh country air.'

'And you? Does it suit you?'

Nash saw the enthusiasm die out of her eyes and sadness creep into its place.

'I feel as if I've come home,' she said quietly, but he knew the homecoming had not been a happy one.

Too many memories of Meg?

He could understand that reason—for him there were too many memories of Russell, but at least he didn't have people pointing fingers at him.

Was his mother right? Had Edenvale made the Marsden twins the scapegoats for their father's shortcomings and its beloved doctor's death?

If so, wouldn't Ella be better finding another country town where Brianna could have an idyllic childhood?

Again he felt there was more going on than Ella would admit, and the suspicion he'd tucked away grew stronger.

CHAPTER FOUR

'I'VE got to feed the dogs.'

Ella headed for the pantry, embarrassed she'd revealed so much of her feelings to Nash—wondering if it had ruined her chances of buying the practice. Right now she needed to be here, needed the work for financial reasons, but also needed access to old town records for the dream.

Once that was achieved, well, she could have moved on—had it not been for Brianna, and Meg's last wish that her daughter be brought up here. Staying on as a locum wasn't an option because Sarah definitely wanted to sell, but would Nash influence that sale?

She couldn't imagine Nash being vindictive. Angry, yes—he became angry easily—but he usually got over it just as quickly.

One way or another, she added to herself, remembering he'd taken Lisa Warren home from the beach barbeque that night…

She opened the bag of dry dog food and scooped some into a bucket.

'Why greyhounds?' a deep voice said, and she realised he had followed her and now he was taking the bucket from her hand.

She let him have it, leading the way to the veranda where Jobba and Priest, the oldest of her three dogs, would be lying in wait for their dinner.

'Meg,' she said, because it would be rude not to answer, then suddenly found she wanted to talk about Meg. 'They were her passion. Not so much the dogs themselves, but saving racing dogs from being put down when they could no longer race for one reason or another. Thousands are put down each year, yet greyhounds are gentle dogs and, contrary to what most people think, they don't need much exercise. They are good companions, especially for children and older people, so it makes sense to try to save them.'

She'd taken the bucket back and was pouring the pellets into three bowls as she explained. Now she turned to look at Nash.

'I didn't foist Girlie on your mother. Sarah met my dogs—Meg's dogs really—and wanted one, and now that Sarah's joined the campaign to save greyhounds, you'll see a lot of them around town.'

Nash shook his head as if he didn't believe a word she was saying, but Sarah was coming up the path and, having heard the conversation, she endorsed it.

'I came to see if you'd like me to mind Pete and Brianna while you go back to work,' she added to Ella. 'I know Mrs Carter is making salads for the fundraiser, so the children can stay with me until it's time to go. I'll take them and you can meet me there.'

Ella shook her head.

'I know they'll be fine with you here, but I don't think you should have the responsibility of minding them at the barbeque. Can you imagine Pete at a barbeque?'

'I'll watch Pete.'

Ella turned to Nash, sure the disbelief she felt was written on her face.

'You?'

He smiled and as her heart did its beat-skipping thing again she realised it wasn't a good idea to make Nash smile.

'I think I could manage a five-year-old without too much trouble.'

'But you're going back to the city.'

Please, let him be going back to the city!

'Not until tomorrow,' he said, smiling again, only this time in a way that made Ella feel distinctly uncomfortable.

And suspicious!

It could only be because he needed more time to persuade his mother not to sell.

What other reason could possibly keep him in Edenvale overnight?

'I'd better see if Pete's awake,' Ella muttered, and she hurried back into the house, anxious to escape both Nash and her thoughts.

Pete, Brianna and Harry were all awake—playing on the front veranda—though Harry didn't seem to be particularly happy that he'd been made the baby in the game of mothers and fathers. He probably knew a baby's bonnet tied to his head wasn't the best look for a dignified greyhound.

Ella smiled, as she often did, when she found Brianna playing. The little girl found joy in such simple things.

'It's time for Harry's tea,' she told them, 'and you two had better have a bath. Then you're going down to Sarah's and she's taking you to the party.'

'But you're coming, too!' Brianna protested, and Ella knelt to explain she would try to get there but she might be late.

Half an hour later, she walked the children across to Sarah's then returned to the house. She had time for a quick shower before she went to work. The dramas of the day were catching up with her, and she wanted nothing more than to soak in a hot bath then go to bed. But she had patients to see and a party to attend. It wasn't enough that she was an active member of the local SES, Edenvale expected its doctor to turn up at such functions.

Melody West was waiting for her at the surgery.

'I'm on my way to the fundraiser, but heard you'd be here so I called to tell you I've tracked down the other four. They're all related and are away at a family wedding up the coast, the men fuming because they're missing the SES party. Anyway, I told the parents what had happened and advised them to take their children to the local hospital and have them checked out.'

'Thanks, Melody. That saves us some worry.'

Ella then explained that she might want to vaccinate the children in the class on Monday.

'Depending on what I hear about the serogroup,' she added. 'The year above this group are all done for A and C, but the younger ones should also have the vaccination. If I give you an information leaflet, could you copy it and send it home to the parents of the younger group?'

Melody nodded, then glanced towards the car park where cars were already vying for space.

'From the look of this, you might not need to send out information leaflets. I know a lot of these cars. They pull up outside the preschool every day.'

Ella looked around and realised there were far more people arriving than she'd anticipated, and as car doors opened and passengers alighted, she knew Melody was right. Word had got around and now anxious parents of young—and not so young—children were flocking to see her.

They'd never fit into the waiting room!

She unlocked the front door, went inside, grabbed a chair and dragged it back outside. Then she stood on it and called out to gain attention.

'If you had an appointment this morning and I didn't have a chance to see you, please go inside and wait. For those of you anxious about meningococcal, if you or your child has a temperature or red spots, you should also go inside and wait. The rest of you, we won't be vaccinating anyone until we know what kind of meningococcal the two children have. That might not be until Monday. If the vaccine I have on hand is the right type, I'll start vaccinating preschool children in Jessie and Carrie's class on Monday. I'll order more vaccine for other people who want it, but I might not get that supply before Tuesday. I won't tell you this isn't worrying, but it's not a cause for panic. So unless you've got spots or a fever, or you're with someone with spots or a fever, go on over to the barbeque and have a good time.'

Some people turned back towards their cars and a few older

patients headed inside, anxious to establish their right to see the doctor.

Ella thought she had things sorted, then a groundswell of noise began, someone declaring their child had as much right to the available vaccine as preschool children, someone else remembering Ella had an interest in vaccinating preschoolers because of Brianna, then more people moved towards the door, determined to do what they felt was best for their children.

'One of the not so good things about small country towns,' someone said, and Ella turned to find Kate behind her. 'News travels fast!'

'You didn't have to come but I'm glad you did,' Ella told her, as the two of them hurried inside before the waiting room was so jam-packed they wouldn't have squeezed through. 'I can't refuse to see the children. Do you think you can sort them into some kind of order? This morning's patients first unless there's someone with a child who's genuinely sick.'

Nash strapped Brianna into his mother's car for the drive to the SES headquarters, which were behind the town sports grounds. He'd given up trying to work out why he'd stayed on in Edenvale, but it was beginning to seem like a bad idea. His offer to mind Pete at the barbeque seemed like an even worse idea—and they weren't at the barbeque yet! The child was definitely hyperactive and, though he wasn't in favour of handing out pills to children without good cause, he wondered why Ella was so adamant he didn't have an attention deficit disorder.

His mother looked up from where she was strapping Pete in on the other side of the back seat.

'You have to remember that because of Carrie's health, she's needed a lot of attention from her parents.'

He peered at her across the top of the car.

'As well as gardening and rescuing greyhounds from death, are you reading minds now?'

She laughed, and suddenly he didn't care why he'd stayed on in Edenvale—he was just glad he had.

'No, but I saw you looking at Pete after you'd caught him climbing onto the shed roof. I could see the thoughts running through your head.'

'He'd only been in the house two minutes. I can't believe he could be so quick.'

'A warning to you for tonight,' she said, as they climbed into the front seats and he started the engine.

'Oh, my!'

His mother made the comment as they reached the end of the drive, but the same thought was in his head and it had nothing to do with mind-reading. The small car park outside the surgery was packed, and people milled about everywhere.

'Just what Ella didn't need!' Sarah muttered. 'People panicking over this wretched meningococcal.'

Nash looked from the crowd to his mother.

'I should stop and help, but there's no way you can handle these two on your own.'

'I won't be on my own,' Sarah said, opening the car door and undoing her seat belt. 'You go and help Ella, I'll conscript some helpers for Pete and Brianna as soon as I get to the party.'

Nash hesitated, but his mother was already around the car and opening the door on his side.

'Go!' she urged, and he got out, but the gladness he'd felt about staying had disappeared. Now he was wondering what the hell he was doing here!

He made his way through the crowd, feeling as well as hearing anger building.

'I don't believe this story about the vaccine!'

'Why should our children have to wait until Tuesday?'

'Remember those cases at a boarding school? The children weren't in the same class at all.'

'Well, I'm going to stay here until my child is vaccinated, and on Monday I'm going to phone the Health Department and complain about Ella Marsden...'

Nash reached the door of the surgery and pushed his way inside—not an easy task considering the crush of people already there. But Kate saw him and waved, relief washing over her face.

He squeezed his way towards her.

'Need help?'

She rolled her eyes.

'I think Ella needs it more. I know with two doctors working, we'd get through this lot faster, but some of these people are angry and ready to be abusive. I don't think it's fair she should face them on her own.'

Nash nodded, remembering too many incidents of angry and sometimes violent patients in A and E.

'I'll join her in her office,' he said, and once again began to make his way through the crowd. He ignored a few calls from people who recognised him, sure Ella would need help, and possibly sooner than she thought.

Her door opened as he approached and she helped an elderly man through it.

'Come out the back way, Mr Stubbins,' she said, leading him towards the rear door. 'You'll avoid the crowds that way, and I'll get Kate to phone you and let you know a time for your next appointment.'

Then she noticed Nash.

'You're supposed to be minding Pete at the party,' she reminded him.

'Mum assured me she could get replacement help. We saw the cars and the crowd and thought I might be more useful here.'

An almost smile was quickly replaced by a frown.

'I'm not vaccinating anyone, if that's what you're thinking you might do.'

He followed her as she ushered her patient to the back door.

'I was thinking more of being a back-up. Kate suggested it. Said some of the patients might get a bit stroppy, and a large male looming in the background might help.'

Now he got a real smile. She shut the door behind Mr Stubbins and turned to Nash.

'It probably would. Maybe I could phone the SES and get them to send someone very large!'

'You don't want *me*?'

He acted hurt and was pleased when Ella laughed.

'Oh, I do, but not as back-up.' The smile faded from her face, disappointing him.

'Do you want me to send them home? I can stand up in front of them and tell them to come back on Monday.'

She shook her head.

'I tried that and it worked for some, but I have to see all those who've stayed, Nash. Imagine if I didn't check them out and someone did have a meningococcal rash! And, worse, how would the parents feel, worrying all weekend about whether or not their child might have a potentially deadly disease? If you could see some of them, that would be wonderful. Same deal as this morning. Anyone who has been in close contact—and I mean close—with Jessie or Carrie should get rifampicin. We'll know the serogroup by Monday, and the vaccine I have in stock has to go to those who've been in closest contact. I'll have more vaccine on Tuesday at the latest for people who want to pay to have their children vaccinated. I'll be working on both the Health Department and local service groups to see if we can get a major vaccination campaign going. Perhaps with help we can cut down the cost, but I can't promise that and it will take time.'

'Have you thought all this through since you arrived and found a riot on your doorstep?' Nash asked, then felt absurdly pleased when Ella smiled again.

'I've thought of little else all afternoon,' she admitted. 'Even when we were talking about your mother or the dogs, I was wondering how best to tackle a possible meningococcal outbreak. I must admit I had the timing of the hysteria a little out. I didn't think people would panic until Monday, especially with the party on tonight, though I guess with their children's lives at stake, why put off panicking?'

They walked down the hall together, stopping where it opened out into the crammed waiting room. Ella lifted two files from the rack and handed one to Nash. She checked the name on hers and called a name, and as she led the patient, an elderly woman Nash didn't know, back towards her room, he called the name on his, and work began.

Again!

'This was the first weekend I've had off for two months,' Nash said, putting first one hand then the other behind his head and stretching his shoulders.

They were sitting in the tearoom behind the reception area, Kate collecting the empty coffee-cups from the table and rinsing them under the tap. The three of them had gathered in the room as soon as the last patient had departed, and without speaking had each fixed their own coffee then slumped around the table. Nash's comment was the first words that had been spoken, and Ella was glad the silence was broken.

At first it had been OK, just unspoken relief that the evening was over, but the caffeine had done its work on her initial tiredness and her brain, at least, was starting to work.

'Mrs Carter phoned to say she'd taken the children home and both were asleep, but she said to tell you she put Pete in your bed.'

Kate relayed this information as she dried the cups. Ella nodded. Pete usually slept in her bed when he stayed over while she…

She felt the flush spread across her cheeks. She'd told Nash she didn't use his mother's side of the house, but she *had* used it. Used the bed in his and Russell's old room from time to time when Pete, or some other of Brianna's friends, stayed over, though she always felt a little sad, thinking of Russell who'd wanted only that Meg love him.

Thinking of Russell because it had still hurt, just a little bit, to think of Nash…

'Thanks,' she said to Kate, then added, 'And thanks for being here tonight. I'd never have managed without you and

Nash, but if you both leave now you can still join in the fun at the party.'

Kate shook her head.

'I wasn't going to go anyway,' she said. 'I'm trying to limit my Christmas activities this year. The last few years I've gone to everything and ended up so exhausted by Christmas Day that it's no fun, while as for New Year's Eve...'

She gave an expressive shrug, but she said goodnight and left anyway.

Ella turned to Nash.

'I meant that thank-you,' she said quietly. 'I *wouldn't* have managed without you. And I'm sorry I've taken up so much of the time you should have spent with Sarah.'

He smiled and, tired as she was, she felt the little hitch in her heart yet again. What had happened to the armour of the past?

'You'd have managed, though maybe not quite as quickly,' Nash corrected her. 'But you were right. You had to see those people.'

He hesitated, then reached out and touched her shoulder.

'Do *you* feel better, Ella?' he asked gently. 'Having seen, what, thirty more children and not found another case of the disease? Will you stop worrying now?'

She tried to smile but failed.

'There are more than five hundred children in this town and we've seen about fifty of them today. That's four hundred and fifty more we haven't seen.'

'But some have already been vaccinated,' he reminded her, wondering why he wanted to reassure her—wondering, even more strongly, why he wanted to hold her in his arms while he did the reassuring.

Because of memories of the past? Memories of her soft young woman's body...?

'That cuts down the numbers,' he finished lamely, far too late for it to seem part of the conversation. Why were his thoughts wandering so erratically? Why did his head keep wanting to rest on the table?

'You're exhausted.'

The sudden accusation jerked him upright.

'And I should have realised it and sent you away,' Ella continued. 'You told me it was the first weekend you'd had off in months. I thought you were making excuses for not coming to visit Sarah, but if you've got the weekend off, you've probably worked all week and, knowing A and E shifts, probably twelve-hour days all week!'

She stood up.

'Come on. If you're not going to the party, I'll walk you up the drive.'

All brisk efficiency, which, fortunately, indicated she couldn't read his mind like his mother could—couldn't know he wanted, for whatever reason, to hold her in his arms.

She locked the front door and they walked through the shadowy darkness, the shush of the waves on the beach far below a gentle counterpoint to the music from the barbeque on the other side of town, the sound drifting towards them on the still night air.

'Can you smell the gardenias? I sit on the veranda at night, and their scent seems to fold around me.'

'Alone?'

He hadn't meant to say that—hadn't meant to spoil the peace that lay between them.

Ella stopped walking so she could turn towards him.

'Yes, alone.' He could see she was puzzled by his question, a half-moon shedding enough light for him to see the frown between her eyes. Then, as if she thought he might need more information, she added, 'Brianna goes to bed at seven and Mrs Carter has her favourite TV programmes.'

'I wasn't thinking of Brianna or Mrs Carter sitting with you. I was wondering about Brianna's father. You're a young attractive woman. Even if he's no longer in your life, there must be someone.'

She turned away, and he was sure she shivered, then, shoulders slightly slumped, she continued walking, scuffing her feet in the gravel on the drive.

'I don't know who Brianna's father is,' she said, and there was so much emotion in her voice—sadness he thought at first, but maybe stress as well—he ignored the shock value of this statement and gave in to the urge he'd had earlier. He caught up with her, put his arm around her shoulders and drew her close.

'I'm sorry,' he whispered, though he didn't know what for—maybe for the thoughts the shock provoked. Then he dropped a kiss on the curls that were escaping from the coil she'd pinned them into, and held her tight against his chest.

They stood for ever, yet he knew it was mere seconds, while the music, suddenly sweeter, wrapped around them and the stars shone brightly though clouds were creeping right across the sky. Ella's body fitted into his as neatly as Pete's jigsaw-puzzle pieces had fitted together that morning, and, tired though he was, the world suddenly became an OK place.

A very OK place.

Then Ella pushed away, turned and walked ahead, and thoughts he didn't want to have crept into his head.

She didn't know who'd fathered her daughter?

Had Ella decided the Marsden twins should live up to their reputation for wildness?

She certainly hadn't been promiscuous back when he'd known her. Her shock that night on the beach when he'd touched her breast had been genuine. But that had been twelve long years ago...

Thinking all these thoughts, he followed Ella without being aware of where his feet were leading him—up the stairs, across the veranda and into the dark, shadowy house.

'Won't Sarah be expecting you?'

Ella's whispered question startled him.

'Oh! Sorry! Wasn't thinking!'

He turned to go back down the stairs but Ella touched his arm.

'Come through the kitchen, it's much shorter that way,' she said quietly, then kept her hand on his arm to guide him through the darkness. But once in the kitchen she turned on the light and he saw the paleness of her face and the almost purple shadows of fatigue beneath her eyes.

'My father usually got a locum over Christmas,' he said, his voice harsh because he hated the pity he was feeling. 'Have you made arrangements to get one?'

She shook her head.

'I was waiting until Sarah decided if she'd sell. If she does, then I'll advertise for a partner and the holidays might be a good time for likely contenders to try out life in Edenvale.'

She gave a very small smile.

'The town has always been much more lively over Christmas, which might give it more appeal.'

'I hardly think you'd want a partner who was looking for a lively life,' Nash replied. 'Surely the way to sell the place is by emphasising the town's tranquillity—suggesting it as an ideal place to bring up children.'

She pushed one of the curls back from her forehead, tucking it behind her ear.

'I was joking, Nash,' she murmured, then she shrugged her shoulders, 'and now I'm so tired if I don't go to bed I'll do like horses do and fall asleep where I'm standing. You can sleep in down at the cottage, but Brianna and Pete will be up at dawn. Brianna considers five o'clock a normal waking-up time.'

He'd been dismissed.

He should go.

But his eyes were on the curl she'd pushed back and which had now escaped again and was falling down over her forehead. He reached out and tucked it back behind her ear, his hand wanting to linger, to finger her ear-lobe and follow the line of the muscle in her neck.

'Goodnight, Ella,' he whispered.

'Goodnight, Nash,' she replied, then she stood up on tiptoe and kissed him on the cheek. 'Thanks again for all your help.'

Now he went. Out the door and down the path towards the cottage, taking long, sure strides because if he didn't get as

far away as possible, as fast as possible, he'd end up going
right back into the kitchen and kissing her...

Not on the cheek...

Ella woke, as she'd predicted, at dawn, brought out of a deep
slumber by two giggling children. They were under the bed
with, from the sound of things, all three dogs and possibly
an elephant as well, the way the bed was moving.

'Oh, dear, oh, dear, there're monsters under my bed.' Ella
put just the right amount of terror into her voice to make the
game successful, but kept her voice low. Mrs Carter deserved
her sleep-in on Sunday mornings.

'What will I do? Who will help me?' Ella cried, as the
movement and muffled giggles grew stronger.

'I'll help you!'

Brave Brianna emerged, a fierce frown on her face and a
small wooden sword in her hand.

At this stage of the game she swiped the sword about under
the bed, and the dogs, if they were present, had enough sense
to get out of the way. But from the yowl of protest, Pete
hadn't dodged, and the game dissolved into chaos as Ella
leapt from the bed to rescue the little boy, praying the swipe
hadn't caught his eye or split his lip.

'Come on, Pete, she didn't mean to hurt you. It was just a
game.'

Ella knelt on the floor, peering under the bed, trying to
coax the cowering child out from under it.

Which was why Nash, having heard the yelps as he'd
walked past the window on his way back from an early morning swim, entered his old room to see a neat behind, encased
in faded blue boxer shorts, protruding from under the bed.

'Trouble?'

His voice startled Ella to the extent she jerked upwards,
hitting her head on the bedframe and adding her own yelp to
the chaos.

'What are you doing here?' she demanded, emerging from
underneath, dragging Pete out with one hand while the other

was occupied with the useless task of trying to tame sleep-tangled curls.

Her face was flushed, and the equally faded blue pyjama top was twisted so he could see far more of her than she realised, and she looked so utterly and intensely desirable Nash was very glad he was wearing jeans. Maybe the man who'd invented them had used strong fabric to prevent male interest in a female being immediately obvious.

'I—er—popped in to say goodbye. I'm heading off after breakfast.' The words sounded incredibly weak, although he couldn't understand why. 'I'm taking Mum up to the city—well, I'm driving her in her car. She knew Charlie when I was at university and I thought she'd enjoy the exhibition.'

Blank incomprehension on Ella's face, but as Pete's bellows grew louder there was no time to explain who Charlie was or what exhibition—or to work out why he'd wanted to.

'He's bleeding,' Nash said, noticing the blood on Pete's hand for the first time.

'Brianna ran him through with her sword,' Ella told him, and he turned to see a very subdued little girl clutching a small wooden sword in her hand.

'Come on, Pete, it's not that bad,' Ella continued, cuddling the child on her lap while two guilty-looking dogs crawled out from under the bed and slunk away. The third had also emerged and was standing guard over Brianna, no doubt ready to defend her should trouble come her way.

Pete stopped crying, Ella dabbed the hem of her pyjama top at a small cut on his hairline and peace resumed.

But the expanse of creamy skin revealed when she'd lifted her pyjama top had caught Nash's attention—and made his jeans even tighter.

What was he doing, lusting after this woman?

She didn't even know who'd fathered her daughter!

He couldn't possibly be interested in Ella as a woman!

The physical reaction must be tied up with…

What?

No sex for a couple of months?

That seemed reasonable.

But he hadn't had lustful thoughts about any of his female co-workers during this celibate time—a celibacy enforced by terrible working hours and Karen's hectic social life, which couldn't be interrupted for something as unimportant as sex.

A view he hadn't even argued over, which should tell him something about the state of *that* relationship.

Ella and the children had long gone, walking past him and across to the other side of the house where Ella would, no doubt, minister to Pete's injury. Calmly and efficiently, Nash was sure.

So why was he still standing in the doorway to his old bedroom, looking at a rumpled bed and sniffing the air, which had changed its texture and aroma since yesterday. His mother would be fixing breakfast, and then they'd leave for the city. Charlie's exhibition opening didn't start until five so he'd have time to call in and see Karen.

But suddenly he knew he wouldn't. Knew he couldn't visit her and carry on as if nothing had changed in his life.

But what had changed?

He didn't know exactly, just knew he had to sort out some things in his mind before he talked to Karen—really talked to her. Her reaction to the meningococcal outbreak had jolted him, but maybe he'd always known that side of Karen—the one that put her interests first—and that he had, until now, accepted it.

He shook his head, unable to believe the weird thoughts he was having. So, he'd stop thinking! About Karen, about Edenvale, about anything! He'd take his mother to the new shopping centre she'd been talking about, browse the shops with her, have lunch, phone Karen to let her know he was back and he'd see her at Charlie's show—he had to do that…

CHAPTER FIVE

ELLA was on the veranda early that evening, waving goodbye to Josh and Pete—and feeling pleased with Josh's report on Carrie's condition—when the phone rang.

'Have you advertised for a partner?'

Sarah's voice!

Ella held the receiver away from her ear, but seeing where the question had come from didn't make it any clearer.

'I can't do that until I know I'm buying the practice,' she said to Sarah, hearing the older woman giggle and wondering if she was tipsy.

'Well, don't,' Sarah told her. 'Not right away. I've found a wonderful locum to work with you over Christmas and then we'll discuss it again.'

Ella's heart sank. It could only mean Sarah had found someone she'd prefer to sell the practice to, and had decided this person would see Edenvale at its best over Christmas.

Feeling physically sick now, she made some kind of noise she hoped Sarah would take as agreement, but as Sarah was positively chortling with her own cleverness—or with tipsiness?—it probably didn't matter.

Ella said goodbye and hung up, then realised she should have asked when this paragon would begin work. With the meningococcal scare she really needed someone immediately, but it was hardly likely Sarah, in the short time she'd been away from Edenvale, would have found an out-of-work doctor ready to start in the morning.

Sarah owned the practice so she had every right to appoint a second locum, but that didn't stop Ella feeling aggrieved.

And very apprehensive!

By morning she was feeling even more apprehensive. Rick

had phoned shortly after Sarah to say he'd followed up on Carrie's tests and the strain was group C. This made things both easier and harder. Easier because there *was* a vaccine, harder because of the work involved in getting first the children then as many other people as possible vaccinated.

She'd sat down at her desk and written a list of the things she had to do, contacting the Health Department being on the top of it. Then she'd made notes of all the ways she might be able to get funding to vaccinate the whole town—or at least everybody under twenty. She'd had to guess the numbers, working from the town's population of twenty-five hundred and general age demographics, but in the end all she'd achieved had been to give herself a headache.

If only she hadn't lost her maths tutor way back then...

Giving it up as an impossible task, she'd gone to bed but she'd no sooner got to sleep—counting adolescents instead of sheep—than the phone had rung again. An elderly patient who suffered from angina, was in pain but couldn't find his tablets. By the time she'd collected some from the surgery, driven to his place, stayed to make sure they relieved his symptoms and to reassure him he'd be all right, it had been a couple more hours before she'd got back to bed.

So it was with dragging feet she made her way to the kitchen on Monday morning, in search of coffee to wake her body up enough to stand upright in the shower. She could hear Brianna chatting to Mrs Carter, the child's voice full of the boundless enthusiasm she felt for life.

'So that's why the little girl's brother got the measles,' Brianna was saying as Ella reached the door.

Why Brianna should be explaining this to Mrs Carter, who'd read the book to her nearly as often as Ella had, momentarily puzzled her, but she didn't give it too much thought, shuffling instead towards the kettle and murmuring a general 'Good morning' to her housemates.

Brianna's greeting was accompanied by a hug around Ella's knees, while Mrs Carter added a scolding.

'You should have slept in a bit longer. I heard you go out last night, that's why I got Brianna up this morning.'

Ella concentrated on spooning coffee grounds into the plunger.

'And I could have taken morning surgery.'

Ella spun around.

Had she walked straight past Nash without noticing he was there?

Without the smallest blip in the smooth beating of her heart?

But her heart was still waking up as well—perhaps that explained it...

'You could take morning surgery?' she repeated, praying there were no holes in her ancient pyjamas. 'Why are you here?'

He smiled at her, and her heart made up for the lack of a blip earlier. Now it blipped all over the place. Blipped, flipped and danced a little! She definitely needed coffee!

'I'm your new locum,' he said, and she realised the smile wasn't a sharing of pleasure but an indication of just how clever he thought he was, dumping this information on her.

'You can't be!'

'No?'

Another smile.

'I think you'll find I can be. Organised it all last night with the woman who owns the practice.'

Smug, that's what he was, while Ella was flabbergasted.

'But you don't want to work in Edenvale,' she bleated. Hell, she hated bleaters—what was wrong with her?

He didn't reply, merely raised both eyebrows, though she could swear there was a glint of satisfaction in his eyes. Or was it a glint of delight at her discomfort?

That was the trouble with glints—it was so hard to tell.

The other trouble with them—in those particular eyes—was that they tempted her to glint right back, to share the delight or satisfaction or whatever it happened to be.

She left the room, coffee forgotten, marching doggedly towards the bathroom where she hoped soap and water might wash away the weird thoughts she was having.

And the suspicions that were building by the minute.

How could she possibly be distracted by glinting eyes when he was obviously here to check up on her?

Working as a locum, he'd be able to gauge how much money the practice made.

No, she was being paranoid—he could ask his mother for the figures.

Did he think she was cheating his mother?

Was he here to check the books were right?

But over Christmas, with all the holidaymakers in town, the practice figures would look much better than during non-holiday periods.

Soap and water didn't help, but it was only when she was dressed for work—sensible three-quarter-length trousers, sensible shirt, hair pulled ruthlessly back into a sensible knot at the back of her head—and heading back to the kitchen that the question she should have asked occurred to her.

OK, his mother had hired him as a locum, but what had Nash been doing, eating breakfast in Ella's kitchen?

'Nash said he'd take me to preschool. He's just gone to get his doctor stuff out of his bedroom. Did you know Nash used to live in this house when he was a little boy like Pete? He was Sarah's little boy. Did you know that?'

Brianna was obviously delighted with her discoveries and Ella hid the nasty clutch of jealousy and told herself it was good for the little girl to have male influences in her life.

But when Nash appeared from the other side of the house, stethoscope in one hand and a slightly battered medical bag in the other, Ella forgot all about male influences.

'You're staying here? In the house?'

Her voice was high enough to be touching hysteria but shock had caused her lungs to contract and a raised-pitch squeak was about all she could manage.

Nash was frowning at her.

'I thought you knew. Mum said you wanted the locum to

live in so he or she could share the after-hours calls. She said—I assumed—I'm sorry.'

At least Nash seemed as put out as she was.

This comforting thought was soon squashed beneath the weighty realisation that Nash would be living in her house, sharing the common rooms, sitting down to meals with her…

'I've got to go now or I'll be late!'

Brianna's tug on her leg brought Ella back to reality.

'Yes, darling, I'm ready now.'

She wasn't—hadn't had breakfast, hadn't come to terms with this enormous change in her life, didn't—

'No, *Nash* is taking me. Kiss me goodbye.'

The pained patience in Brianna's voice restored some of Ella's equilibrium, and she lifted the child into her arms and gave her a kiss and a hug.

'Be good, and make sure you put your seat belt on.'

Ella looked at Nash across Brianna's curly head, unable to voice all the concerns she had.

'I'm a safe and steady driver,' he said, not a glint or hint of a smile in his eyes now.

Ella put Brianna down and watched as the little girl put out her hand trustingly to Nash.

Just as she had given her hand, and then her heart, into Nash's keeping, only to have it returned.

It hadn't been her heart he'd wanted…

In spite of her suspicions, having Nash had made a hectic day far easier. Ella hadn't admitted it to him just yet, but she would. She was sitting with her feet up on her desk, working up enough energy to go out and thank the staff for the great job they'd done.

Nash had deferred to her from the start, and had gone with Carol, the practice nurse, to the preschool, vaccinating not only the children in Carrie's class but the younger ones as well, so all preschool children and all aides and teachers had now been done.

Marg, her weekday receptionist, had done her usual job and

a bit of Carol's as well, helping out with dressings and fetching things for Ella, while Kate, co-opted back on duty, had spent most of the day on the phone with the Health Department, drug companies and service club representatives, questioning and explaining, trying to get whatever help was available for a town in trouble.

'Kate tells me you've a third case of meningococcal but it's unrelated to the other two.'

Ella swung her feet back down to the floor, feeling the heat of embarrassment flooding into her cheeks. What would he think of her, sitting there with her feet all over his father's desk?

And would she ever get used enough to this situation that her heart wouldn't react every time he walked through the door?

'Yes to the new case, and you're right on the unrelated aspect—he's fourteen and, as far as I can tell, has had no contact with either of the girls.'

She was exhausted, not so much from work but from trying to work out where to go next.

'What bothers me is the vulnerability of teenagers. Did you know it's the most important infectious cause of death in fifteen-to nineteen-year-olds? Everything I read and hear seems to suggest teenagers are far more likely to have severe consequences from the beastly thing. I've ordered more vaccine and we'll start on all the high-school kids tomorrow. I've phoned an agency for another nurse—two nurses should be able to handle it.'

He'd grabbed a chair, turned it around and was straddling it, his chin propped on his arms, which were folded across the top of the backrest.

'Rifampicin?'

Ella sighed.

'I want to give it to anyone who's been in contact with the latest victim. I've permission to use his name—it's Rhys Carter, Mrs Carter's grandson—and have asked the local radio station if I can have five minutes just before the news.

I'll explain what's happening and ask people who've been with Rhys at school, or sporting fixtures, or parties, to come and see me at the surgery, free of charge. I'll open up again at seven to see them. Jeff's got more supplies of the rifampicin, so anyone who's been close to Rhys can take a course.'

'If Rhys was at the fundraiser on Saturday night, you're talking about most of the people in town. Do you think going public is wise?'

Nash was thinking of the panic on Saturday night. Tonight they could be here until midnight!

Ella offered him a tired smile—the kind of smile that prompted all the wrong thoughts in his head.

'I know we risk panic spreading again, but I think it's time, not to panic but to…'

She looked at him, hazel eyes pleading for him to find the word she needed.

Or the solution she needed?

Then she shrugged.

'To get serious, Nash. I want this thing stopped now, not in a week's time when some other child might be a victim.'

Nash nodded, hearing the passion and commitment in her voice.

'OK by me,' he told her. 'So, what's the plan?'

This time her smile was slightly brighter.

'I'm abdicating as the maker of plans,' she said. 'Kate yelled at enough people at the Health Department for them to agree to send down one of their top epidemiology experts. Rick Martin, a paediatrician who now works full time on the cause, effect and control of outbreaks, in particular meningococcal, should be here in the morning. He'll tell us the plan.'

Nash frowned at her.

'If this man is coming, shouldn't he be the one going on air?'

Ella smiled again, a teasing effort this time.

'In case they shoot the messenger?'

'Something like that,' Nash admitted. 'But he would also

be able to give more information about what's likely to happen next. As you said, he's the one who'll be making the plan.'

Ella considered this for a moment, then shook her head.

'No, I want anyone who's been in contact with Rhys—and anyone we've missed who's been in contact with Jessie or Carrie—on antibiotics as soon as possible. Rick can do a wider coverage on the local segment of the TV news tomorrow, but in the meantime I'll do tonight's appeal.'

'I'll come with you to the station. In fact, I'll drive you.'

Nash wasn't sure why he'd offered, and neither, from the wary look on her face, was Ella. But she didn't argue, which suggested she must be as tired as she looked.

'I've got to thank the girls for all their help, then go home and see Brianna before I leave.'

She got to her feet and walked towards the door, then swung back to face him.

'Thank you, too, Nash. It would have been impossible to achieve as much as we have today without you here.'

'It was my pleasure,' he said, and found he meant it, although he wouldn't class jabbing needles into three-, four- and five-year-olds as most people's idea of pleasure. Neither had his afternoon session, seeing some of Ella's patients, been one hundred per cent fun. Old Warburton had come in, and hadn't been in the room three minutes before Nash realised he had been there to check out what Ella had already prescribed for his condition. Check out Ella's competence as a doctor.

Rotten old sod!

But by the fourth patient he'd realised why he was enjoying himself. It boiled down to the luxury of time—having time to talk to the patients and, better still, time to listen to them, really listen, as Ella must have listened to Mr Warburton that she'd cunningly persuaded him to try antidepressants!

Much as he liked A and E work—and had thrived on the adrenalin rush of it—there'd been no time for people, only for patients.

He followed Ella out to the waiting room where she was still thanking the staff as she waved them goodbye.

But as the last of them disappeared out the door, her shoulders slumped and he saw how tired she really was.

'What time do you have to be at the radio station?'

She didn't reply, looking instead at her watch as if it might sort out an answer for her.

It obviously did, for she eventually raised her eyes to his.

'Forty minutes. It's still in the centre of town, opposite the beach, so I've time to pop home and see Brianna for a few minutes and maybe grab a shower, freshen up a bit.'

'It's only radio—no one will see you,' Nash reminded her.

This time her smile was wide, and genuine, lighting up the hazel eyes and wiping some of the tiredness from her face.

'No, but the broadcasting booths are small and pity help the person stuck in close confines with me if I don't have a shower. It's been one heck of a busy day.'

Nash smiled right back, and then, because it seemed good to be with Ella, both of them smiling at each other, he took the keys from her hand, put an arm around her shoulders and guided her out the door.

Her body had stiffened under his touch, but it wasn't until he had to concentrate on getting the deadlock locked that she moved away.

Probably for the best. The way his body was behaving around Ella, touching her was not the most sensible of moves.

Distance—that's what he needed.

Was a metre enough?

They were walking up the drive towards the house, a good metre apart, yet he could still feel the hardness of her shoulder blade beneath his hand and the softness of her body when he'd held her last night.

'Nash! Nash! I've been waiting and waiting for you.'

Brianna hurled herself off the veranda, down the steps and along the drive, eventually grasping his leg to stop her forward momentum.

'It's my turn for Show and Tell tomorrow and I told my teacher I'd bring you.'

'Good grief, do they still have Show and Tell?'

Nash directed his question at Ella, who was kneeling down to kiss Brianna.

'They do,' she replied, then she said to Brianna, 'I don't think you can take people to Show and Tell. I think you take things.'

'Kirsty took her brother who broke his leg,' Brianna told her, then turned all her attention back to Nash. 'I said you were Sarah's boy and all the children want to meet you—because of the boy in the garden, you see.'

Ella saw Nash's frown and realised he had no idea what Brianna was talking about.

'You haven't seen much of your mother's garden, have you?' she said, trying hard not to sound censorious. 'Sarah transformed it into a special place for children and all the preschoolers have been invited to play there from time to time. Right down the back there's a statue of a little boy, and the children call him Sarah's little boy.'

'But that's not necessarily me,' he said quietly. 'In fact, for Mum it's more likely to be a reminder of Russell—when he was young and well.'

She heard the sadness in his voice, but no anger—though at the time of Russell's death he'd been so angry he'd accused Meg of killing his brother.

'Manic depression is a terrible thing,' she said gently. 'As bad as some forms of cancer, I always think, because there's no real cure, just the hope that maybe medication can keep the worst of its effects at bay.'

She spoke quietly, not wanting Brianna to hear the conversation and ask questions, but the little girl was telling Harry about Nash doing Show and Tell, so had missed it.

Nash nodded, though the look on his face suggested her words had been cold comfort, then he diverted the conversation back to where it had been.

'Why would the children call the statue "Sarah's little boy"?'

Brianna was back between them again, and Ella reached out and touched her head, the knowledge that she couldn't protect this precious child from either cancer or mental illness or any other risk life held tying her stomach in knots. She breathed deeply to calm herself and answered Nash's question.

'There was some confusion early on. A child was playing too close to the statue and a teacher called out to be careful—to keep further away from Sarah's little boy.'

'So that's why all my class want to meet you,' Brianna told him. She seized his hand. 'Say you'll come.'

'Please!' Ella reminded Brianna—the word coming out automatically. But Nash must have thought she was adding her own plea for he looked at her.

'Why should it matter to you?'

Her tension eased and she laughed and shook her head.

'The "please" was for Brianna, not you. I'm going in to have a shower before this conversation gets any worse.' She paused then added, 'You *can* say no to Brianna, if you don't want to go. She understands the word, and she also knows that she can't have everything she wants.'

She hurried away from them, disturbed now not by fears for Brianna but by how enjoyable it felt to be laughing with Nash. Enjoyable was worse than the inner responses she was feeling in his presence. Enjoyable couldn't be explained away as a physical hangover from her youth.

Enjoyable was downright dangerous...

Nash watched her disappear into the house then sat down on the front step and faced the smaller version of the woman who was confusing him.

'Can you only do Show and Tell tomorrow, or could I come another day?'

Brianna studied him for a moment, then asked, 'What other day?'

He smiled at the question. This wasn't a child who was going to be put off indefinitely.

'Maybe Wednesday,' he offered. 'Because of the meningococcal—the disease your friends have got—I will probably be very busy tomorrow.'

'You might be busy Wednesday as well, and Show and Tell only lasts ten minutes. Our teacher has a clock with big hands and a bell that rings so when the hands go together the bell rings and you have to stop.'

'OK, I'll go tomorrow,' Nash agreed, and was surprised when the little girl flung herself into his arms and wrapped her arms tightly around his neck. He smelt the soft perfume of her hair and felt the curls tickling his chin.

'Thank you, Nash,' she whispered, then as quickly as she'd appeared she was off again, up the steps and into the house, calling out to Mrs Carter, anxious to share her news.

Nash listened until the childish voice disappeared, then he stood up and made his way around the house towards the cottage. He'd have time to say hello to his mother before he went back out again. The way things were panning out, who knew when he'd have another chance?

But as he walked past the kitchen he heard Brianna's voice again and remembered the feel of her chubby arms around his neck. He felt a sense of…not loss exactly, but maybe lack, although up till then he'd never given much thought to having children of his own.

His mother wasn't in the cottage, so he ventured into the garden for the second time, this time following a path beneath overhanging branches and through an arch hung with crystal prisms that threw rainbows of colour on the pebbles beneath his feet.

He saw the statue of the little boy before he saw his mother, who was kneeling at the edge of a garden, trimming dead flowers off a bush.

'Brianna told me about the little boy you have here,' he said, sitting down on a seat beneath an arbour of white roses. 'Russell?'

His mother stood up and studied the statue for a moment.

'I don't think so,' she said, though she answered slowly as if she was still trying to work things out. 'I saw him in a garden shop and thought how well he'd suit this particular spot, but after I'd brought him home I wondered if perhaps he'd had a look of Russell and that's what had caught my eye.'

She was frowning at the statue, then she shook her head.

'I don't think so. I often look at it but I can't see any resemblance. It's just a boy, and I really like him here. But the gardening itself has helped me get over it at last—get over Russell's death. It's been my therapy—a bit delayed but better late than never.'

She studied Nash with the same intensity.

'Does it still hurt for you to think about him, Nash?'

He gave her question the attention it deserved, mentally poking into the places where his hidden bruises were.

'Not as much.' The admission surprised him, and he found himself explaining it. 'At first a lot of the grief was mixed up with guilt. I was the elder—his big brother. I should have been able to help him, protect him, save him.'

'None of us can do that for each other,' his mother said quietly, coming to stand beside him and putting her hand on his arm. 'Not even for our children,' she added, and he knew she understood exactly what he felt.

CHAPTER SIX

HE WALKED back to the big house, had a quick wash, then waited on the veranda for Ella to appear.

In jeans tonight, the denim faded, not, he had a feeling, by fashion but by wear. But all age had done to them had been to make sure they fitted snugly to her neat backside, while the turquoise shirt she wore didn't hide the soft curves of her upper half.

What was wrong with him that he was thinking such thoughts? The town where he'd grown up—the town he'd told this very woman he cared about—was under siege from a potentially fatal disease and he was thinking about his colleague's neat butt.

'I thought I'd start off by saying we were already getting help from the Health Department and all measures were being taken to stop the meningococcal spreading further, then explain it isn't passed on easily but ask anyone who's been in close contact with any of the three victims in the past week to come to the surgery for a check-up.'

They were walking down the drive to the garages behind the surgery where both their cars were now housed, and she laid out her plan, her voice anxious, as if she needed some back-up or approval.

'You'll just say check-up, not mention the antibiotic?'

She hesitated.

'I've changed my mind so many times about that, but in the end decided on check-up. If people think they can get the antibiotic, we'll get another mad rush like last night, and for one thing, I hate giving antibiotics unnecessarily because both people and bacteria can build up a resistance to them, and, although Jeff got more in today, we don't have enough for the whole town right now and I want to make sure the people who need it most get it first.'

Nash could find no fault with her reasoning, though he did find fault with the way her perfume, or perhaps it was a faint scent from her hair, was twining around him, so his thoughts switched between rifampicin and bodies and butts.

They reached the garages and he led her towards his car, opening the passenger door for her, smelling the hint of scent again as she slipped past him into the seat. But by the time he joined her, she was the one doing the sniffing.

'I love the smell of leather!' she said, snuggling deep into the soft seats. 'My car smells of wet dog.'

Nash glanced towards the ancient four-wheel-drive he'd noticed earlier. She was probably still paying off university debts and would be going deeper into debt to buy the practice, and he supposed children didn't come cheap, even when they were as small as Brianna.

But still…

He caught the thought before it went any further, backing the car out and reminding himself that not all women thought the way Karen did. Her belief was that doctors had a certain standing in the community and should both dress to show it and drive cars that suited it. He hadn't really needed to see the car. One glance at Ella's clothes would be enough to dispel any idea she might share Karen's views.

Ella sank back into the comfortable seat, relaxing more than she'd thought would have been possible in Nash's company. She glanced towards him, able to study his profile as he concentrated on the road, wondering what he was thinking and whether he was remembering other times he'd driven her places.

'I think you're right!'

Of course he wasn't thinking about other times he'd driven her places!

'About not mentioning the rifampicin?'

'Yes. Last night was just a preschool panic. Imagine the dimensions of a whole town panic!'

He turned and smiled at her and for one foolish moment she regretted the suspicions that still hovered in her mind. Regretted the past as well. How good it would be to have Nash, her friend, who'd tutored her in maths, back again— Nash before that first, life-altering kiss.

She shivered as she remembered the strange and wondrous feelings that kiss had awoken in her, taking her from child to woman in a single bound, without the maturity she'd needed to handle womanhood, or a mother to guide her along the path.

That kiss and the ones that had followed it…

'So, who's the local newsreader these days? Some bright young thing, or does Col Hampton still rule the roost?'

'Col's still here,' Ella replied, as Nash pulled into a parking area at the local radio station. 'He doesn't seem to get any older. I thought he was old when I was growing up, but old might have been late twenties to me then, so he'd only be in his forties now.'

'Has to be.' Nash had come around the car and was holding the door open, but Ella was reluctant to get out—reluctant to be so near him when her memories had taken her to dangerous places.

She forced herself out of the car, then, so close she could see his face clearly in the well-lit parking area, she asked the question she hadn't wanted to ask.

'Why are you here, Nash?'

His eyebrows rose

'Driving you to the radio station?'

'No, here in Edenvale, working as a locum. Do you want the practice for yourself or do you just not want your mother to sell to me?'

'Is there some reason we're having this conversation right now?' he asked, his mouth tightening as if angry that she dared to question him. 'Don't you have an appointment with a radio mike?'

She walked away, wishing she'd been wearing shoes and

not sneakers so her cross footsteps would have stamped across the paving.

He didn't follow her, which meant she could relax slightly before tackling the announcement she had to make, and Col's friendly greeting relaxed her even more.

Until he introduced her, told his listeners she had something to say, then announced the station would run a phone-in session in the morning, and if they wanted to ask Dr Marsden any questions, that would be the time to do it.

'A phone-in session?' Ella echoed, when she'd said what she had to say and Col had switched to the national news and she could talk to him without the whole of Edenvale hearing her.

'Brilliant idea, don't you think? It only occurred to me after you'd phoned, and I would have run it past you before you went to air, but you were cutting it pretty fine. I made it six in the morning because at that time only people who genuinely want answers will be up and about—or will drag themselves out of bed. You won't get as many nuisance callers.'

'Well, thanks!' Ella muttered at him, then glanced at her watch. It was after seven and she'd said she'd be opening the surgery at eight for anyone who was worried. If tonight was going to be as bad as Saturday night, she needed food before she tackled the hordes.

Nash was leaning against his car when she emerged from the building.

'That went well.'

'You listened to it?'

'Cars do have radios, you know! You didn't tell me about the phone-in—isn't six in the morning pushing things a bit?'

'It wasn't my idea, it was Col's. I didn't know about it until I heard him announce it. He claims I won't get as many nuisances at that time.'

'And you won't get much sleep, if tonight's as busy as Saturday.'

She had to smile.

'I've just been thinking that myself. Well, I'd better grab

a bite to eat before the onslaught. You could leave me here. I'll get something at the café and walk back up the hill.'

'Leave you here? Why should I? I need to eat, too, and then I'll be going to work with you.'

She looked at him and shook her head, suddenly very tired as well as totally confused.

'You don't need to work tonight. I doubt it will be as bad as Saturday. I can manage.'

'Rubbish. You've got a locum to help out, so let him help out. Come on, we'll go to Shastri's, have a proper meal then face the hordes together. And I'll do calls tonight as well. If you've got to be up at the crack of dawn, you'll need your sleep.'

Ella hesitated but he was already holding open the car door and her mouth was watering at the thought of one of Shastri's delicious curries. But as they drove to the headland opposite Sarah's house, where Shastri and her family lived and ran their popular Indian restaurant, the question he hadn't answered loomed up again in her mind.

'I know why I've got a locum,' she said, 'what I don't know is why you're it. And don't give me any rubbish about it being your mother's practice. That you're here at all means you've either taken leave from your hospital job or are on holidays—one's not easy to arrange, and the other's not very sensible to give up, so there has to be a reason, Nash, and I'd be stupid if I wasn't suspicious.'

He didn't answer, his attention on the road again, but when he pulled up in front of the restaurant, he parked so they could see the sweep of Edenvale Bay and the wide, wine-dark ocean stretching into the darkness.

'Maybe it's because of this,' he said, waving a hand towards the magnificent view. Then he got out of the car and, not wanting to have him opening the door for her again—standing close—Ella clambered out as well. Then she peered back in, patted her pockets and cursed quietly.

'I can't go out to dinner,' she told Nash, forgetting all about the conversation they'd been having. 'I wasn't thinking of anything more than going to the radio station. I haven't got any money on me.'

'I'll buy you dinner,' he offered. 'Or if that offends your sense of locum-boss relationships, I'm sure Shastri's would let you have one meal on credit.'

'I don't do credit!' Ella told him, and Nash saw her lips tighten and wondered just how badly her father's behaviour had affected her. The old car? Bought with cash because she refused to take out a loan?

She'd be the only doctor in the world without one, he was sure. Right from their days in medical school banks and credit unions offered loans to medical students.

'Then I'll pay and you can pay me back, or shout next time.'

'Why would there be a next time?'

She was as prickly as an echidna!

'Because we'll be working together for the next month, and there'll be patient matters we need to discuss and it's nice to be able to discuss things over dinner occasionally. Less formal than in the surgery.'

She was walking with him towards the restaurant entrance but he could see suspicion in the stiff way she moved.

'I won't be able to afford Shastri's very often,' she said, her voice quiet and somehow hurt, and again he wondered what had really brought her to Edenvale. Something more than she was saying, that was for sure.

Was she in debt to someone?

Hiding?

'When Brianna and I go out, it's usually to the mini-golf—they do a mean hamburger there.'

Nash shook his head, unable to believe this beautiful woman—and she *was* beautiful—counted a visit to mini-golf with her daughter as a high point in her life.

So, why didn't she know who'd fathered that daughter?

No matter where his thoughts went, they invariably circled back to this question.

And just as invariably came up against the realisation that there was something decidedly iffy about Ella Marsden's presence in this town.

He hadn't answered her question about why he was in Edenvale, which led Ella to believe her assumptions had been correct. But it hurt her to think Nash felt the need to check up on her—hurt her deep inside the dark places in her heart where the Nash she'd loved still lurked.

But as she breathed in the sea air and felt the cool evening breeze ruffle her hair, her love for the town where she'd grown up came over her so strongly she knew she'd fight to stay here—fight for Brianna's right to grow up in Edenvale—whether the enemy was Nash McLaren or the entire town.

Straightening her shoulders, she strode towards the restaurant. And she'd reorganise her budget so that the pay-back dinner for Nash was held right here. She wasn't going to have him think she was a tightwad.

Or skint!

Which she usually was, but that was because of the plan...

'Oh, Ella, lovely to see you.'

Shastri, for whom the restaurant had been named, greeted Ella with a warm hug. They had been at school together and had been friends. Misfits joining up together, Meg had always said, as Shastri's family were the first Indians to settle in Edenvale.

Ella returned the hug, then held her friend at arm's length.

'And what's your news?' she asked, seeing a glow of happiness in Shastri's eyes.

'It's Serif. He proposed.'

Shastri held out her left hand, showing Ella and Nash, who'd followed Ella in, a ring with a dazzling ruby set in diamonds.

'But you were always going to marry Serif,' Ella protested. 'It was arranged when you were children—before your family came to Australia.'

Shastri smiled again.

'Ah, yes, but marriage isn't always about love, is it, Ella?

What is magical for me is that we fell in love. I fell in love with Serif and he with me.'

Ella shook her head.

'Don't you believe in love?' Nash whispered in her ear as they followed Shastri to a table on the veranda with a view out over the ocean.

'Love to order? Like that?' Ella whispered back, but when Shastri left them to peruse the menu she added, 'I'm glad for them, of course, but it does seem strange.'

'Any stranger than other ways of falling in love, Ella?' Nash asked, looking up from the menu to watch her face as he asked the question.

And she remembered him taking off her glasses, and even before that first kiss she'd known she was in love...

So she didn't answer—couldn't answer—and couldn't read the menu either because her reading glasses were with her money in her handbag back at the house.

She tried holding it at arm's length but when that didn't help she put it down, deciding she'd ask Shastri what the specials were and settle for one of them.

'I'll read it out if you like,' Nash offered, and she looked up to see him smiling at her, as if he knew not only about her still needing glasses but about the strange way she'd fallen in love.

Discussion of the next phase of their war against the spread of meningococcal got them through the meal, and by the time they returned to the surgery—Kate again there to help—there were so many patients waiting that they had no time for further conversation.

The last patient finally departed.

'No more suspicious spots on the ones I saw,' Nash said, and Ella nodded.

'Same here, thank goodness.'

'Coffee?' asked Kate, and Ella shook her head.

'I've got to be at the radio station at six tomorrow morning, and I haven't walked the dogs all day, so I think a turn around the headland then bed for me. But Nash might like coffee.' She turned towards him. 'Kate has a key and can lock up— actually, I should give you a key in case you need something from the storeroom for a night emergency. I can't believe you've been here a whole day and I haven't shown you around properly.'

'The circumstances have been slightly out of the ordinary,' he reminded her, 'and, no, I won't have coffee, but I'll join you for that walk if I may. I think I need some fresh air to clear my head after all the arguments I've had with anxious parents about antibiotic prophylaxis.'

Kate pursed her lips in a silent whistle, and Ella glared at her. She'd have liked to have told Nash she didn't want his company on her walk, but the headland was public property and he could walk there whenever he liked.

Though preferably when she wasn't!

So once again they walked up the drive together, only this time they didn't talk so there was no need for her to sound fraught and no excuse for him to give her a comforting hug— and that's all it had been—and no excuse for her to lean on him and think seductive thoughts about how nice it was to be in Nash's arms again.

She whistled for the dogs, and as her three came bounding from the house she led them towards the side gate, which would take them onto the parkland that stretched across the headland.

'They don't have to be muzzled?'

'Not in this state,' Ella explained. 'It's an old law and it does still apply in Queensland—I'm not sure where else. Not that it's a hassle. In the city, some people feared the dogs, so Meg used to muzzle them for walks.'

Which finished that conversation, Nash realised. He wondered what he could ask next, or what conversational gambit he might introduce. He had to find something—and fast— because walking on the headland with Ella was bringing back too many memories.

They'd walked just so as teenagers, only then they'd held

hands, and had stopped to kiss occasionally. He'd realised, soon after their first kiss, that kissing had been very new to Ella, but she'd been only to willing to explore the novelty in some depth, so they'd walked and kissed and walked again.

'Did you go on seeing Lisa?' The question, not from him but from Ella, startled him with its prescience. 'I mean, she was your year—went up to uni at the same time—did you go out with her there?'

Nash tried to remember. First year university, he'd gone out with so many girls, though mostly he and his friends had hung around in groups—groups with girls included, but not formally pairing off, not 'going out' as such.

'I saw a bit of her but, no, there was never a big thing between us.' He'd answered before he'd thought of the question from the other side, and now he stopped, watching the dark shadows of the graceful dogs chase across the grass. 'Why did you ask?'

She turned towards him and smiled.

'I suppose because of where we are. Walking the headland at night. I only ever did that on my own or with you, so I guess my memories led me to the question.'

Moonlight revealed a slight smile playing about her lips, but it made her eyes look sad. An emotion he couldn't put a name to gripped Nash's heart, squeezing it as if to drain the blood from it.

And because he didn't want emotion coming into his dealings with Ella—he wanted to find out what she was up to in Edenvale and why she wanted his father's practice—he let anger burn away the other, unidentifiable emotion and went on the attack.

'You don't walk here with Jeff? Enjoy the moonlight on the water, and *his* kisses?'

She looked hurt, and then she shrugged.

'Don't walk with me again,' she said, and, whistling for the dogs, she turned away, taking long determined strides back towards the house. But he caught her easily, grasping her shoulders and turning her to face him. The dogs were far enough ahead to not realise what was happening, and Ella, he realised, was too startled to protest.

So he bent his head and kissed her. Kissed her hard. Demanding a response he knew she didn't want to give, only gentling his lips when she did respond, her tense body relaxing against his. Years melted away and he was eighteen again, kissing Ella in the moonlight on the headland, the sea breeze flirting around their hot bodies, catching in their lungs when they gasped for breath.

'I'll walk with you again,' he said when she finally pulled away. 'If only to find out what you're really up to, here in Edenvale.'

She stared at him and, though the moonlight wasn't all that bright, he could see the confusion in her eyes. But the dogs were jostling him away and this time when she walked on, he let her go. Maybe another brisk walk across the headland might clear some of *his* confusion.

Ella was gone before he was up the next morning, but Mrs Carter had heard the broadcast and declared Ella better on talk-back radio than most of the radio hosts who demanded and were paid enormous salaries.

'But I felt sorry for her when things got personal,' Mrs Carter added, dishing two eggs and enough bacon for an army on to Nash's plate. 'Someone asked if she wasn't Tom Marsden's daughter and whether the money he'd pinched from the people of Edenvale had paid for her to be a doctor.'

Nash swore under his breath and felt his stomach churn. Did Ella put up with this kind of abuse often?

His breakfast was suddenly unappetising, but he cut a piece of bacon and chewed it carefully.

'What did she say?' he asked Mrs Carter, wanting to push the food away but knowing he'd offend her if he did.

'She said she was here to answer questions about a potentially deadly disease and could callers please stick to that.'

He wondered if her voice had quivered as she'd said it, or

if she had held strong. He was beginning to believe there was a lot of strength in the grown-up Ella Marsden.

'I smell bacon.'

Brianna erupted into the kitchen, her curls more or less controlled in two bunches, one on either side of her head.

'It's Nash's bacon,' Mrs Carter told her. 'You have cereal for breakfast.'

'Sometimes Ella lets me have bacon,' Brianna said, speaking so wistfully and looking so longingly into his eyes that Nash almost clapped the performance.

'Then I suppose I could let you have a piece of mine,' he said, noticing for the first time that Brianna called Ella by her name, not the usual Mum or Mummy. 'Do you want it on toast like a sandwich?'

Brianna had pulled her chair close to his and had settled on it, and was now eyeing his breakfast with a gourmand's appreciation.

'On toast, please, with just a little bit of the egg.'

'Brianna!'

Mrs Carter's protest was met with a delightful smile.

'Just one morning, Mrs Carter,' the young minx said, holding up one finger.

'Just one morning, all right? I know you.'

But the housekeeper was smiling too and Nash saw pride and affection in that smile and realised how much joy this one small child had brought into both his mother's and Mrs Carter's lives.

He made the sandwich carefully, certain Brianna would tell him if he got it wrong, and had just cut it into small squares and put it on a small plate in front of her when hurried footsteps echoed through the house.

'Any chance of coffee, Mrs C.?'

'Ella!'

Brianna was off her chair and flying to the kitchen door, where she flung herself at Ella's legs.

'Nash made me a bacon sandwich, with a little bit of egg, from his very own breakfast.'

Ella had lifted the child into her arms for a kiss and a hug and now looked at Nash across her shoulder.

He saw the hurt in her eyes, only slightly diminished by the obvious joy she felt at holding Brianna, and he wanted to go to her—to hold them both.

As if!

He'd killed off any closeness that might have been growing between them last night. Best he stick to business.

'How did it go?'

She shrugged and set Brianna down on the floor with advice to eat her sandwich while it was hot.

Mrs Carter had poured coffee for her and set the cup on the table. She poured another cup for Nash then bustled out of the kitchen, muttering something about getting the washing on, a transparent excuse to get away before she was asked for a comment.

'I answered a lot of questions, one from a mother whose daughter—a high-school student—has spots. I said to bring her straight in. They live on a property out of town so I knew I'd have time for coffee and to say goodbye to Brianna before they got here.'

'I hope you're having more than coffee for breakfast!' Nash scolded.

'Nash will make you a bacon sandwich,' Brianna offered, and Ella smiled.

'I had cereal earlier. I'm not stupid, Nash, I know I have to eat.'

She'd picked up her coffee and carried it across the room. Now she leaned against the bench beneath the windows and sipped at it, the morning light finding glints of gold and amber in her curls—still wildly free, unrestrained from their usual, businesslike coil.

But the sunny curls only emphasised the sadness of her face and the dejection in her posture.

Was she still hurting from the caller's innuendo?

Did she have to deal with such accusations often?

And, if so, why on earth would she want to remain in Edenvale?

Why not find some other quiet country town in which to bring up Brianna?

'I make good bacon sandwiches,' he said.

CHAPTER SEVEN

IT WAS almost a relief to have a patient with a real problem, though the gash on Henry Abbott's leg was nasty, and badly infected.

'I don't suppose it occurred to you to come in when you did it,' Ella scolded him.

'Couldn't,' came the laconic reply. 'We were forty miles out in the bush, cutting some old red cedar trees. Power people are putting new lines through the area, and they'd just bulldoze the trees and red cedar's a mighty pretty timber.'

Ella led Henry to the treatment room, calling to Marg to send Carol in.

'I'll anaesthetise it then leave you here with Carol. She'll clean it out so we can see what's what.'

She helped Henry up onto a table and injected a local anaesthetic into a number of sites around the wound. She'd need it numb before she stitched it, and as the cleaning process would be painful, anaesthetising it now would save Henry some pain.

'Chainsaw?' she asked, as she examined the jagged edges more closely.

He nodded, and Ella cringed, thinking how easily the deadly blade could have sliced off his whole leg.

Carol arrived, and Ella left her with the patient, returning to her room to find Nash waiting there.

'I thought you might be relieved to know your out-of-town patient with the spots has beard rash.'

'Beard rash?' Ella repeated, trying to ignore her reaction to the delighted smile on Nash's face.

'You know, that redness from kissing someone with a few hours' growth. Apparently she's recently discovered boys, the best—and presumably the most physically developed—of whom catches the same bus home. Hanky-panky in the back seat of the bus, Ella. You can't have forgotten the stories of what went on on school buses.'

'But none of that was true!' Ella protested, all but blushing when she remembered some of the stories she'd heard in her high-school years.

Nash laughed, and touched a finger to her cheek—so probably she *was* blushing.

'Not all of it, but I've no doubt there's always been a bit of kissing—in fact, I saw evidence of it this morning. The girl—it was Kylie Wilson—either didn't know her loved one's ten-hour shadow could scratch her skin, or she wasn't happy to tell her mother she'd been kissing, so blamed meningococcal.'

Ella felt a lot of the tension she'd been carrying since that morning's broadcast drain from her body. She even managed a chuckle at Kylie's predicament.

'Did you see her without her mother? Tell her what it was?'

'See her without Mrs Wilson? You've got to be joking. There was no way Mrs Wilson was going to leave her Kylie in a room with a male doctor. At first she insisted she see you, but I suppose worry got the better of her. Anyway, I told her it was just a rash and to use a soothing cream on it, but I managed to grab Kylie as they walked out and warn her not to kiss boys with stubble.'

'I'm glad, and thanks for telling me. I do "chat with" sessions at the high school every couple of weeks, just sitting in the sickroom, available to any pupil who wants to ask questions or talk about a problem without going through the hassle of an appointment. I'll look out for Kylie at the next one—hopefully she'll come and see me.'

'In case she needs contraceptive advice?' Nash asked, and Ella shrugged.

'Any relationship advice, though it has to be do as I say, not do, as I do kind of help. I'm not a shining star as far as relationships go.'

Nash wanted to ask more, but Ella's phone was ringing and he knew there were hordes of patients in the waiting room.

He walked away, but not before hearing gladness and relief in Ella's voice as she said, 'He's here! Oh, thank heavens!' Then she whisked past him in the corridor, rushed through the waiting room and all but threw herself into the arms of a tall, blond man who had, from the look on Marg's face, been flirting with her until Ella had appeared.

After kissing the stranger—well, pecking him on the cheek but giving him a far too enthusiastic hug—Ella turned, speaking to the man, gesturing and looking truly happy for the first time since Nash had been back in Edenvale. Then she took him by the hand and led him towards Nash, who was standing in the entrance to the waiting room, a patient file in his hand but the name on it still unread.

'Nash, this is Rick Martin. He's a specialist from the Health Department. He's the one who'll make the plan!'

OK, so it was natural she'd be pleased someone had arrived to shoulder the bulk of the responsibility for the outbreak—but hugging pleased?

Hugging pleased meant she knew the bloke!

Knew him well!

Relationship well?

She was still talking, leading both men towards her consulting room.

'All the papers are in here,' she was saying. 'Kate has set out the patient files and also drawn up lists of the patients we've already treated, other patients who'd already been vaccinated earlier and all the contacts we could find for the three who've been positively diagnosed.'

She turned to Nash.

'I've a patient in the treatment room. Would you mind going through all this with Rick?'

'No, you do it, I'll take your patient. What's the problem?'

'Chainsaw cut. Carol's cleaning it and I've anaesthetised

the area,' Ella explained succinctly, though she still looked worried.

'I do that stuff in A and E all the time,' Nash told her, but her frown didn't go away, so that wasn't what was bothering her.

He had a closer look at Rick Martin, but apart from the fact it confirmed the guy wasn't particularly good-looking— OK good-looking but not movie-star material—it didn't tell him much.

Except that he was standing very close to Ella, so if body language counted...

'The patient's waiting,' Ella reminded him, then she led Rick Martin into her consulting room.

Nash remembered old Henry Abbott from his childhood, when timber cutting had been the second-largest industry in the town, the local sawmill employing nearly as many people as the dairy co-op. They talked of the old days as he stitched the jagged cut. Then he checked Henry's tetanus status—up to date—prescribed antibiotics and let the old man go, reminding him he'd need to come back in a few days to have the dressing changed.

Rick Martin was back in the reception area, sitting at a desk, papers spread out everywhere, speed-reading them by the look of things, as he was jotting notes and highlighting text at an astonishing rate.

Ella must be seeing a patient, and though Nash felt he could pop in, making an excuse of telling her about Henry, he knew he had to get on with what he was there for—seeing patients.

By one, the waiting room was empty and, more importantly in Ella's view, no new cases of meningococcal had bobbed up. She walked through to where Rick was working and found Nash already there, sitting at the desk beside Rick, reading through his notes.

'So, what's the verdict? Do we panic?'

Rick turned and smiled at her.

'We go to lunch. Nash was telling me there's a great restaurant up on the headland just out of town. How about I take you there?'

Ella smiled and shook her head. Rick loved good food and going out and doing lunch, but lunch with Rick involved long, leisurely discussions of the menu, consultations with the waiting staff, sometimes even hobnobbing with the chef.

And wine!

Rick didn't believe a meal was a meal without wine.

'How about I send out for sandwiches, and all three of us share them right here while you tell us what to do next?'

His face fell, but Nash looked pleased, though it was none of his business whether she lunched with Rick or not.

'I suppose that'd do,' Rick said reluctantly, 'but I'll expect you to have dinner with me tonight! We'll go to the restaurant then.'

'And deny Brianna the pleasure of having dinner with Uncle Rick?' Ella teased, and Rick shuddered and held up his hand.

'I love that child, Ella, I truly do. You know that, darling. But eating with children? You know my views on that subject!'

Only too well, Ella thought, but she was too pleased to have Rick there to worry about the past. She turned to Marg, asking her to order sandwiches for lunch, then made herself a cup of coffee. The urn was there if Nash wanted one, and as Rick didn't drink anything but a brew made from his own special beans, freshly ground and filtered, she didn't bother asking if he wanted one.

Thankfully it was Tuesday and afternoon surgery didn't start until three, so by two-thirty, the three of them, with Rick's guidance, had worked out a plan to vaccinate all children and young adults under twenty-five over a three-year period.

'These are the most urgent ones,' Rick had said, highlighting the high-school children and the rest of the under-fives in town. 'The Health Department will do them. I'll try to get a bus down here later this week, with staff and vaccine. I'm doing an interview for the local television news tonight—my secretary organised that yesterday—and the department will put notices in the paper. You have supplies of vaccine now, so you can let patients know—the ones who don't fit the criteria to get it free. I'll mention you have it in stock—that it's available if they want to pay for it.'

'It's expensive and with the dairy industry in trouble a lot of the townsfolk can't afford it,' Ella told him.

Rick shook his head.

'We're doing the most vulnerable, Ella—for the rest, it's up to them.'

He pushed the papers aside, stood up and checked his watch.

'They're pre-taping my interview at three.' He looked down at her. 'Want to come? We can do a double act.'

Ella shook her head.

'Far better you go on your own,' she said. 'Seeing me on TV might put people off.'

Rick laughed as if she'd made a joke, but Nash heard the pain in her voice and knew she was remembering the question from the aggressive caller that morning.

'OK! Then what about dinner? We'll go to the restaurant on the headland?'

The man wasn't going to be put off, and Nash, with only a slight churning of his stomach, which might have been from the salmon sandwich he'd eaten, watched Ella and waited for her answer.

It came as a sigh, then a falsely bright smile for the visitor.

'I'm sorry but I've got an SES meeting tonight and, really, do you need to stay? We have the plan, so once you tape your interview, you can go back to the city.'

'Sending me away again, Ella?' Rick asked, and though he smiled the easy, teasing smile that seemed to be his trade mark, Nash heard dissatisfaction, and maybe even pain, in his voice.

'You walked away, Rick,' Ella said, tilting up her chin in a gesture Nash was beginning to recognise as a prelude to a fight. 'Something about not being able to take to ankle-biters, wasn't it?'

She stood up, picking up her empty coffee-cup and carrying it towards the sink. Rick followed her, and Nash watched as the Health Department man slipped an arm around Ella's slim waist and whispered something in her ear.

If he pushes her to go to dinner with him, I'll belt him one, Nash thought, then shook his head. He never had even *mildly* violent thoughts before.

He saw Ella shake her head, then the man had the hide to kiss her on the neck. Though Nash was sure he saw Ella stiffen before she moved away from him, she said nothing more than, 'Thanks. You've been a great help.'

Rick returned to the table, gathering up all the papers and his notes.

'Let me know if you have another case,' he said, as much to Nash as to Ella, then with a general goodbye he left.

Ella turned to wave him—not seeing him out the door as she did even with patients—then swung back to face the sink. No way could it be taking her that long to wash a coffee-cup. Was she upset?

Crying?

The thought of Ella crying brought thoughts of violence back to Nash's mind, but he couldn't see her shoulders moving.

He stood up, found a dirty cup Marg or Carol had left behind the reception desk and took it across to the sink.

Ella wasn't crying, but she was rubbing at a non-existent mark on the outside of the cup—rubbing and rubbing.

'Old friend, is he?' Nash said, hoping he sounded casually disinterested when what he really wanted to do was to take Ella's hands in his to stop the rubbing, draw her close and hold her in his arms.

He wanted to tell her everything would be all right, although he had no idea what was so wrong.

And maybe, a little later, kiss her. Not as he had last night, in anger, but gently, persuading her response from her rather than demanding it...

She put down the cup before he could put any of these ideas into action—fortuitously perhaps—then she walked away, gathering up the notes Rick had left for her.

'It was another life,' she said, and Nash wasn't sure if she was answering his question or talking to herself.

'One you miss?' he asked, deciding he may as well assume the words had been meant for him.

'It's none of your business, Nash.'

'None of my business? When you're trying to persuade my mother to sell you the practice? What do you intend doing? Staying here for a while—building up the figures—then selling at a profit so you can go haring off back to the city to a man who seems to think more about his stomach than about you? To a man who's apparently admitted he doesn't like kids? What about the patients? People who've put their trust in you? What about Edenvale?'

He knew he'd gone too far when she responded with one of the saddest smiles he'd ever seen.

'I don't think Edenvale would miss me,' she said, surprising Nash, who'd expected her to fight back. Then he remembered what Mrs Carter had told him about that morning's caller and wondered just how deeply it had wounded Ella.

But before he could say something—anything—to atone, she added, 'Any more than Rick does.'

She walked away, and it took a few seconds for Nash to react, but when he did he followed her, straight into her consulting room.

'You can't say things like that and walk away,' he protested. 'Not and look so sad. What happened? Did you love him? Did he hurt you?'

Now Nash wanted to go after Rick Martin—murderous intentions once again raging in his normally placid heart! He told himself to calm down, to stop behaving like an idiot, to think before he opened his big mouth.

But he didn't listen.

'Is Brianna his? Is that what happened? He obviously doesn't want a child in his life. Did you decide to go ahead with the pregnancy in spite of his wishes?'

Ella looked startled for a moment, then frowned fiercely.

'Nash,' she said, almost gently, though there was pure steel beneath the words, 'This is not the time or place to be having this discussion—in fact, there's no time or place to have it. My life, past or present, is none of your business.'

She seemed about to say more, but the loud wail of a siren ripped through the air, the noise rising and falling like the wail of a wounded animal. A very large wounded animal!

'I've got to go,' Ella said. 'You'll have to start afternoon surgery on your own. With any luck the call will be something minor like a grass fire and I won't be needed. In that case, I'll be straight back.'

She hurried to her desk, picked up her black bag, opened it and began to check the contents.

'That's the SES siren—don't you wait until you're called?'

'I'm an SES volunteer as well as a doctor,' she explained. 'Volunteer numbers are so low at the moment, they'll take anyone.'

She flashed him a smile.

'Even five-foot six, weak and feeble females.'

She was gone before he remembered why the words she'd quoted were so familiar. He'd remembered teasing her with them at one time, telling her, when he'd joined up, that the SES was men's work.

Then he remembered something else. Something more recent. Ella talking to Rick—something about denying Brianna the pleasure of eating with Uncle Rick, something else about Rick not liking ankle-biters. Of course Brianna wasn't his! How could a pretentious number-cruncher like Rick Martin have fathered a lovely child like Brianna?

'Ella gone?' Marg asked when he wandered back out to the waiting room to find the receptionist back behind her desk.

'Yes,' was all he could manage, for he was already worrying about what disaster might lie in wait for the not so weak and feeble female with whom he was working.

'Well, at least we've got you here to take over the patients. She usually only does night calls for the service but, with Christmas holidays and a lot of people away, we're down to a skeleton crew of volunteers. Of course, they all managed to stay for the party on Saturday night. Funny how they can make it to the party but not be here when there's a crisis.'

'Why are the numbers down?' he asked Marg, wanting to know more, worrying that the emergency service was so short of volunteers that the local doctor had to be an active member.

'A lot of the old members, the men who started the service, all retired at about the same time. That led to bad management for a few years. Blokes fighting over who'd be captain. Then a lot of the new people in town come from the city where services are provided. They give money and go to the bar-beques in support, but it wouldn't occur to them to go to weekly practices or climb into a uniform and get up on some-one's roof to spread a tarp when there's a storm.'

'City folk!' Carol added, coming in on the tail end of the conversation, but by now the waiting room was filling up again so Nash set aside thoughts of what Ella might be do-ing—at least there was no storm so she shouldn't be teetering on the ridge capping of a roof—and concentrated on the pa-tients.

He was showing Mrs Horwitz out, having spent most of the consultation listening to the latest gossip, and only a very small part of it listening to her asthmatic chest, when Ella reappeared, bursting through the front door, still in her baggy, bright orange SES uniform, the silver reflective tape glinting under the waiting-room lights.

'It was a grassfire up on the headland so I got the truck to drop me off here, rather than go back across town for my car,' she explained, but whether to Nash or to the remaining patients he didn't know.

She was unpeeling the overall as she spoke, stripping off the hot, heavy garment to reveal her sweat-soaked clothing beneath. Then, with the pile of orange around her feet, she sat down on a chair in the reception area and pulled off a pair of heavy boots.

'Damn! Didn't think about my shoes. They're back at the station.'

'You've got your "going out" sandals in your bottom desk drawer,' Marg reminded her. 'You can wear those if you think going barefoot might detract from your doctor's image.'

Ella smiled her thanks. Nash saw her tired, flushed face light up, and noted the way her damp garments clung to her slim but shapely form. He felt his body stir and wished he was still wearing jeans.

'Mr Grayson, if you don't mind me being barefoot for a few moments, would you come through?' she said, and Nash realised he'd been standing watching her instead of doing his own job, calling his own patient.

And Marg was watching him—watching him watching Ella!

They finished afternoon surgery only half an hour after the appointed time of five o'clock.

'Something of a record,' Marg remarked.

'Having two doctors makes the difference,' Carol said. 'Now, if we can just persuade Ella to hire someone to do the bills and paperwork, she might get to have a normal life.'

'She doesn't have a bookkeeper?' Nash asked, surprised because even back in his father's time, when the town had been a lot smaller, there'd been a woman who'd come in four days a week to do the bookwork and pay the wages.

He thought of the old car, the far from new clothes, and wondered again about Ella's financial situation. Had she been saving frantically so she could buy her own practice?

Was she reluctant to borrow money because of the debts her father had run up, then swindled the co-op to repay? At least that was the story, though Nash vaguely remembered his mother saying it was through careless, drunken stupidity more than dishonesty that Tom Marsden had lost the money.

He was considering that when Ella whisked through the waiting room, collected her SES overall and heavy boots, then headed for the door.

'If I don't go right now, I won't have time to play with Brianna before the truck picks me up for the meeting tonight. Marg, can you lock up? Oh, heavens, did we ever give Nash a key?'

This last remark was also addressed to Carol. Nash may as well not have been standing right there.

'You go, I'll give him one,' Marg told her, but Ella saw Nash wave away the offer.

'I've got one from Mum. I'll walk up with you, Ella.'

It was the last thing Ella wanted. Seeing Rick again had swept her back to the terrible time when Meg had died. It had been bad enough, having her memories jostling in her head, without Rick suggesting they should get together again and Nash questioning her private life.

Then, on top of that, she'd been shocked to realise Nash thought Brianna was her child. Actually, something he'd said some other time—yesterday?—about Brianna's father had puzzled her, but she hadn't realised his mistake. A natural mistake, now she thought about it, though she'd assumed Sarah would have explained things to him.

Did it matter?

She shook her head. She didn't think so. Couldn't think of any reason why it would.

'Are you having a long, involved conversation with yourself that your lips are moving and you're shaking your head?'

Nash had reached out and lifted the overalls off her arm and was now taking her boots from her hand.

'I can carry them!' Protesting was easier than answering his question. 'And tonight, do you mind taking any calls until I get back? It's just a normal training session so I should be back by ten.'

'What do you normally do about calls when you're at the SES?'

'Switch the phone through to my mobile and go from there in all my orange glory.'

She smiled, remembering old Mrs Cranston demanding to know why she was dressed like a man. 'We don't get many night calls—or we didn't. I think people realise that with only one doctor in town, you only phone in a real emergency. And there's always the ambulance. If you're having a heart attack the ambulance is the best option as they arrive with all the life-saving equipment and the staff are all paramedic trained.'

They were talking about nothing—well, almost nothing— and Ella wondered if Nash was as aware of it as she was.

Did he feel they were just words passing between them to cover the other stuff that was happening? Or was it only happening to her? Were the tendrils of excitement that walking near him caused purely one way?

Of course they would be! He'd moved on from *her* twelve years ago. He had a girlfriend—one who had been around for years, according to Sarah.

But that kiss last night had felt real…

Brianna was waiting on the veranda and, seeing her, Ella remembered something that would take her mind more effectively off Nash and kisses than the work conversation had.

'I forgot to ask you. How did Show and Tell go?'

Nash stopped walking and turned to look at her.

'I imagine, from Brianna's point of view, very well. From mine?'

He smiled and Ella forgot all the reasons Nash wasn't interested in her as her heart throbbed in her chest and her stomach scrunched excitedly.

'I think we lost the ''Sarah's little boy'' plot somewhere along the line. Might have had something to do with Brianna announcing that I was living in the house with her and you, just like a real daddy.'

Ella felt heat sweep into her cheeks, and the protest she attempted came out as a strangled kind of gurgling noise.

'Exactly!' Nash said, striding on ahead, up the steps and onto the veranda, dropping Ella's clothes on a chair then lifting Brianna high in the air and swinging her around, before kissing her on the cheek and setting her back on the ground.

He then turned back to Ella who was standing, apparently turned to stone, at the bottom of the steps.

'So you see,' he said, as Brianna ran to greet Ella, 'it *is* my business what you're up to!'

CHAPTER EIGHT

SOMEHOW Ella got through the week, or through until Friday afternoon. She'd avoided Nash as much as possible—or avoided opportunities to be alone with him, taking advantage of having a second doctor in the town to spend more time with Brianna.

Jessie and Carrie were both doing well, while Rhys, who'd been Ella's biggest worry, was out of hospital. The Health Department staff in their bus had vaccinated hundreds of children, while dozens more had been brought to the surgery, anxious parents willing to pay to protect their children.

So it was with a clear conscience she'd left Nash to see the remaining patients and collected Brianna from preschool, taking her to the library, one of Brianna's favourite places, and settling her in the children's quiet reading and play area, before heading for the section where local records were kept.

She'd begun her search at the council chambers, then had contacted various government departments, only to find, to her surprise, copies of all the annual reports of the now-defunct dairy co-op had been passed over to the local library. For the past few weeks, whenever she'd had some spare time, she'd been photocopying them, collating the pages and setting them aside, wanting to have all the information before she began trawling through it for what she needed.

'Marg said I might find you here.' She turned to see Jeff Courtney standing behind her at the photocopying machine. 'I was wondering if you'd have dinner with me tonight.'

The prospect of not having to eat dinner at the same table as Nash was enormously appealing, but Jeff had been asking her out ever since she'd returned to Edenvale, and although she'd accepted his invitations a few times, she knew it was a relationship that would never go anywhere as far as she was concerned, and it was unfair to lead Jeff into believing it might.

She sighed, and concentrated on turning to the next page she wanted to copy.

'It's not such a hard question,' he said. 'It's just dinner. I'm not going to whip you off to some secluded spot and make wild passionate love to you.'

'More fool you,' a deep voice said, and Ella looked up to see Nash standing right behind Jeff, though how he'd got so close in the few seconds she'd been distracted, she didn't know.

'Yes, I'd love to have dinner with you,' she said to Jeff, turning her photocopied pages over so Nash couldn't see what she was doing. He was far too fond of poking his nose into her business.

'Afraid you can't,' Nash told her. 'That's why I'm here. The SES co-ordinator phoned with a message for you. The weather bureau is predicting rain and storms for next week, beginning Sunday, so they've switched the night rescue practice from Monday night to tonight.'

He propped himself against the wall next to the photocopier, no doubt hoping to see whatever she'd been copying when she removed it. Then he folded his arms and regarded her with a smug smile.

The word 'gotcha!' seemed to hover in the air.

Ella ignored him—mentally, if not physically—and smiled at Jeff.

'Tomorrow night?' she said, then felt an absolute worm as his face lit up.

But it fell again almost immediately.

'Oh, no, I'm working. Now the school holidays have started, all the stores in town go into late-opening-for-Christmas mode. By the time I've checked the tills and locked up, I won't finish until nine-thirty or maybe later.'

Nash gave a huff of what might have been derision and Ella glared at him. She considered offering to bring a picnic supper to the shop, but knew that would give Jeff the wrong idea and she'd only be doing it to spite Nash.

'Well, maybe I can call in and see you there,' she said. 'Brianna and I have been making Christmas decorations, and I thought we might hang some of those striped candy canes from the tree as well. I think I saw some in the shop the other day.'

Jeff assured her he had striped candy canes and other edible decorations as well, then he departed, leaving Ella with the photocopier and Nash.

'Don't let me keep you,' she said, and she wasn't talking to the photocopier.

'I've got nothing else to do,' the irritating man said. 'Maybe I can help you.'

'No, I've finished,' Ella told him, glad it wasn't a lie. 'But you could go and find Brianna for me if you like. She's over in the children's section.'

'Well, you know where that is,' he said, as smooth as silk. 'Why don't you go over and get her while I put your books away.'

Ella's heart was pounding—from Nash's closeness, from this stupid, falsely polite exchange, and from trepidation he'd see what she was doing.

Though why the last should worry her, she didn't know—except that the plan had always been for it to be a secret and a surprise.

'I'd better put them back. Librarians are very picky when people put things back in the wrong place.'

She lifted the lid of the photocopier and slid the thick report out, glad she had it doubled over so he couldn't see the cover. Then she set it, face down, on the others, gathered her papers together and, holding the reports and her photocopies, went in search of Brianna.

Nash could hardly follow her around the library. Or not for long, anyway.

Not thick books, Nash mused as she moved away from him. But something she didn't want to share. He kept telling himself he was wrong to be suspicious of her, but then something like this would happen, or he'd go into her consulting room and see her sweep a pile of papers hurriedly into a drawer.

Something was going on in Ella Marsden's lovely head, and he intended to find out what. Quite apart from natural curiosity and a desire to protect his mother—and the whole town if it was exceptionally nefarious—trying to suss out Ella's secrets stopped him thinking about her physical attributes and the way they were affecting his body and interrupting his sleep.

'Nash! I found a book on caves.' Brianna, who seemed to have only two speeds, flat out or dead stop, hurled herself towards him. 'Do you know about the caves right here in Edenvale? Ella took me and Pete into the big ones, but she says we can't go into the little ones until we're older. Do you know our caves were made from lava and they're really lava tubes and lava— What's lava again, Ella?'

She turned, obviously expecting Ella to be behind her, but clever Ella must have slipped away to return the books she'd been copying.

'Lava is the hot stuff that flows out of volcanoes,' he told Brianna, taking the book she was offering him and looking at the pictures of caves.

'But we don't have volcanoes in Edenvale,' his young informant reminded him.

'We did millions of years ago,' Ella offered, appearing from the direction of the children's section.

Could she have been photocopying something as innocent as a children's book for Brianna? Or maybe some ideas for her Christmas decorations?

Nash studied her face and saw a flush in her cheeks, and what looked very much like guilt in her lovely eyes. No, he didn't think she'd been photocopying ideas for Christmas decorations!

He followed the pair towards the counter, where Brianna checked out her book.

'I've got my car, if you're hanging around, thinking we need a lift,' Ella told him as they walked out the front door.

'I knew that,' Nash told her, although he hadn't given the matter any thought. In fact, if someone had asked him, he wouldn't have been able to say exactly why he was hanging around.

Because he liked being near her?

'Pshaw!'

'What did you say?'

He could have sworn he hadn't said it—not that it meant anything anyway.

'I wondered where the rescue practice was tonight. If the service is short on volunteers, the least I can do is put my hand up while I'm here. I can do as you do when I'm on call and switch the phone to my mobile. I used to belong, back when I had long university holidays, so I've done all the basic training. Done helicopter rescue training as well.'

Ella was looking at him as if he'd suggested they should go dancing naked down the main street. Hmm. Dancing naked with Ella somewhere appealed! Dear heaven, had he said that out loud?

'I don't think you can rejoin just like that. I mean, there are papers to fill out—insurance and all. There'll be a business meeting in a fortnight—you could rejoin then, only by then it won't be worth it as your time will be nearly up.'

She was gabbling and she obviously knew it for her cheeks had coloured quite deliciously. But she'd also managed to remind him that his time in Edenvale was limited and it was the feeling that reminder gave him, rather than his attraction to Ella's pink cheeks, that needed consideration.

He walked her to her car, Brianna hopping and skipping between them, turning her head up to ask Ella a question, and something in the movement, or the profile of her face, reminded him of his mother.

'It's interesting, the question of heredity and environment, isn't it?'

Ella turned towards him with a frown.

'Now, where did that come from?' she asked, turning away again to unlock her car, her neat backside stretching her tired jeans as she lifted Brianna into her car seat.

'Brianna looked like Mum there for a moment,' Nash explained, knowing that now he'd started this conversation he'd have to finish it, even if his mind had been diverted along other tracks. 'It must have been a gesture or movement that she's picked up in Mum's company—environment, you see.'

He stumbled to the end of the lame explanation, distracted now because Ella was staring at him, the colour gone from her cheeks, leaving her as pale as the bleached beach sand behind her. Then she turned and peered at Brianna, as if checking she had the right child.

'Could it be?'

She said the words so softly Nash knew they weren't meant for him, but they intrigued him nonetheless. Had she seen some resemblance in her daughter that she was now attributing to her interaction and close relationship with Sarah? It *had* to be that!

But as Nash walked towards his car, the other interpretation that could be put on Ella's words trampled destructively through his mind. Of course Russell wouldn't have had an affair with Ella! If ever there'd been a one-woman man in the existence of the entire male species, it had been Russell and that woman had been Meg.

But Ella looked like Meg!

Could they have swapped?

No! Even the worst things he could ever imagine Ella or Meg doing—and he'd been able to imagine plenty back when he'd felt guilty about the way he'd treated Ella—he couldn't see them doing a swap joke on Russell.

But perhaps had Ella comforted him some time?

Physically?

But if she had, wouldn't she have remembered it?

Again the thought of Ella having so many lovers she didn't know who'd fathered her child kicked him in the guts.

Damn the woman…

*   *   *

Ella drove home, forcing herself to watch the road, not to keep turning around to peer at Brianna in search of a resemblance.

She thought back instead to five years ago—to where she and Meg had both been in their lives. Meg had finished her studies and had been working in the suburban practice, dreaming of one day returning to Edenvale, sending her sister money from time to time, because in that, Ella's final year, she'd stopped her part-time work to concentrate on study.

Had Russell been around?

Ella gave a huff of laughter, though the sound held more sadness than joy.

Russell had *always* been around! Caught in a hopeless love for Meg that, try as she might, she had never been able to return. But neither had she had the heart to tell him to stay away from her. And Russell had settled, or had said he'd settled, for friendship if that's all she'd had to offer him.

Had Meg finally given in to his persuasion? Offered him the solace of her body because she couldn't offer him love?

Ella could feel her frown deepening as she tried to put the pieces together.

Knowing she'd be going out again shortly, she drove up the drive and left the car at the bottom of the front steps. By the time she'd opened the back door, Brianna had unstrapped herself from her seat belt and was ready to clamber out. But Ella lifted her, holding her close, studying the features that had always just reminded her of Meg.

She shook her head. Nash was imagining things. But as she put Brianna down and the little girl turned to say something, Ella saw what Nash had seen earlier. A look of Sarah!

Environment! she told herself, but as she followed Brianna up the steps—far more slowly—she pondered what a can of worms would be opened up if her niece *was* Sarah's grandchild.

An unscrupulous person could use it, a devil deep inside her head suggested. If Sarah knew, that would clinch the sale, no matter what objections Nash put up.

But wasn't she here to clear the Marsden name, not add more mud to it?

She carried the papers she'd photocopied through to her room and added them to the pile she kept in Meg's old brief-case beneath her bed, but as she latched it up she rubbed her fingers across the leather.

'Oh, Meg,' she whispered to it. 'Why did you have to be so secretive about it?'

But even as she asked the question, she knew the answer. Meg's dream had been to return to Edenvale, to bring Brianna up in the town—but only when the money had been repaid and the Marsden name had been cleared. Only then, Meg had felt, would she have been truly happy.

And only then, Ella thought sadly, would Meg have felt she could present Sarah's granddaughter, untainted by the past and her mother's name, to her.

It could all be nonsense, Ella reminded herself as she shoved the briefcase back under the bed.

But she knew it made more sense than anything else, which left her with a dilemma she didn't know how to begin solving!

Ignoring it seemed the best idea, so she showered and changed, then wandered down to Sarah's garden, knowing Brianna would be there.

The pair were sitting on the garden seat beneath the bower of roses, close to the statue of the little boy, and as Ella approached she could hear Brianna 'reading' her book on caves to Sarah, whose arm was around the little girl's waist and whose eyes gazed with pride and affection at the child.

'Can't you see it?'

Nash's whisper spun Ella around—and straight into denial.

'Nonsense!' she said, but she knew her cheeks were be-traying her. Why on earth couldn't she tell a simple lie with-out blushing? 'You're imagining things!'

'Like I'm imagining there's no way you'd not know the father of your daughter?' he growled. 'You nearly had me there, Ella, but once I saw the resemblance I knew why you'd lied to me when you said that. Knew there's no way you could have changed so much you'd had indiscriminate sex with so many men you wouldn't know who Brianna's father was! But Russell? Was it a joke between you and Meg? Did you pretend you were her?'

He paused, then added in a low, silky but dangerous tone, 'Or pretend Russell was me?'

He moved closer and she knew that if his mother and Brianna hadn't been nearby he'd have kissed her—hard and hot as he had kissed her on the headland. And Ella's stupid body actually ached for that kiss, while her mind, which should have been sorting out how to tell him Brianna was Meg's daughter, had gone on strike, thinking only of the heat that seemed to burn in the air between the two of them— thinking of combustion…

The wail of the siren splintered the air and adrenalin rushed through Ella's system, then she remembered it was a practice. She moved forward, explaining to Sarah and Brianna she had to go, telling Brianna to be good for Mrs Carter.

'I'm staying at Sarah's tonight,' Brianna announced. 'Mrs Carter is going to visit Rhys, and Sarah said Nash was going to take you out to dinner and I could stay at her place. And in the morning we're going to make special biscuits to hang on our Christmas tree—like real decorations, only you can eat them.'

Wide eyes looked pleadingly into Ella's.

'Please?'

Ella looked at Sarah, whose nod confirmed the invitation was official and whose pleased look suggested she was only too happy to have the child stay overnight.

'Thanks,' Ella whispered, once again overwhelmed by Sarah's kindness and generosity. She leaned forward and kissed Brianna goodbye, then kissed Sarah's cheek as well.

'Thank you,' she murmured again. 'For everything!'

But as she walked away her head was bent, her conscience yelling at her that Sarah deserved to know Brianna was her granddaughter—if that was the case…

She was so caught up in the impossible situation she failed to register Nash right behind her until he spoke.

'Shall we go in my car tonight?'

She spun towards him.

'We're not going out to dinner, no matter what you told your mother. I know I owe you a dinner, and I'll buy you one, but I've got an SES practice on tonight. That's what the siren was for, stupid!'

She flung the words at him, angry though her anger was at her own confusion not at him.

'I know that. I'm the one gave you the message, remember?'

He was so smart-mouthed she *could* now be angry at him, but before she could let rip he was speaking again.

'And I told you I'd come with you. I've switched the phone through to my mobile, and I've checked with Bob it's OK.' He paused, knowing he'd got her, then added, 'Bob is the SES captain, isn't he?'

Ella wanted to bite him—hard! How she could ever, for one second, have considered kissing him again she didn't know! He was the most aggravating man on earth.

Too furious to answer, she stomped into the house, grabbed her overalls and boots, then went out onto the veranda.

'You didn't answer about the car,' Mr Infuriating said, following right along behind her. 'You can sniff the leather in mine.'

'And it'll do well over the rocks on the road to the caves,' she snapped. 'We're not going into the tourist part but into the lower caves tonight. It's a practice rescue because we always have a lot of cavers here during the holidays, and where there are cavers there's always a risk of an accident.'

They'd reached the car and she opened the back door of her old four-wheel-drive and flung her gear inside, then was startled to find Nash touching-close beside her, taking the car keys from her hand, announcing he'd drive.

It's my car and I'll drive, Ella wanted to yell, but she was trembling so much, whether from Nash's closeness or from the stress of that afternoon's revelations, she knew she'd be unsafe behind the wheel.

Which didn't make his assertive attitude OK, and later, when she could think straight, she'd tell him so.

But it was a long time before she could think straight. They reached the designated rescue area ten minutes later, to find that most of the crew already assembled and she'd been elected as the victim in the rescue.

'You're the smallest and lightest,' Bob explained a little apologetically, as he handed her a safety helmet with a light on the front of it. 'And though we know we could have to rescue big solid men from the caves one day, there's no real need for us to be getting hernias in a practice, now, is there?'

Ella accepted her role with fortitude, clambering into her overalls, pulling on her boots, then sliding down the rope into the first of the caves that lay below the headland south of Sarah's house. At least as the victim she didn't have to carry rescue equipment.

The lava flow that had formed the caves had been less forceful here, so the caves were smaller—low, rounded tunnels burrowing towards the sea. On this headland, one had run close to the surface and erosion had worn part of the roof away so there was a hole that led down into it.

'We're going west towards the hills. I've chalked marks on the wall so follow them, then drop to a lower level when you've gone about sixty metres.'

Bob yelled his instructions from the top as Ella and her rescue team set off, their big torches lighting the blackness of the caves, the light from their headlamps glimmering on mineral deposits left in the walls.

'Dropping down here!' Mark, the rescue team leader, told her, shining his light to where the tube had collapsed onto the one below, leaving a mound of rock and rubble with a small opening that led to the lower level.

Tight spots like this appealed to cavers, who seemed to need an element of danger in all they did. And they'd enjoy even more the drop to the floor of a much larger tube once they were through the boulder choke, as cavers called the rubble.

Mark squeezed through beside her and let down a rope ladder he'd been carrying.

'Remember, both hands and one foot on the ladder at all times, and keep your weight on your feet, not your hands and shoulders.

Once satisfied the ladder was secured at the top, he sent Ella down. She reached the bottom safely and moved out of the way of those following, noticing a pool of water to one side of the tunnel. Were these pools called sumps?

'At least we can stand upright now,' a familiar voice said, and Ella realised for the first time that Nash was in the rescue party.

'Not for long,' Mark responded, before Ella could demand to know what Nash was doing there. 'We're going west again, then through a crawl space and down into the lower cave. We won't, for the sake of practice, traverse the water down there or go into the small tunnel that leads into the cathedral cave, but it's in that small tunnel that people have got stuck or panicked and not been able to move. I think you'll find the crawl space bad enough if you're at all claustrophobic.'

Ella heard the word and shuddered. She didn't think she was claustrophobic but she'd never had a lot of opportunity to find out. Mark took the lead now, and she followed him, aware of Nash right behind her—wondering why she hadn't been aware of him earlier.

Unless he'd deliberately walked at the back of the rescue crew, which maybe he would as a new member.

Thinking of Nash, she followed Mark into the crawl space,

aware how limited it was for her and wondering how all six feet of Nash would squeeze through. Thinking both the town's doctors shouldn't be however many feet they were underground!

'Don't worry, I've done it dozens of times. Bob and I were going to be world-famous cavers at one time.'

She was sure she hadn't voiced her worries, but as she crawled—or, more correctly, wriggled on her stomach—through the narrow space, using her elbows to pull herself along, she felt strangely comforted to know that Nash was right behind her.

Once through they dropped down again, this time on a rope, then equipment that had been dragged through the crawl space was also lowered, some team members remaining on a ledge where the crawl space opened into the cave.

Ella turned so her torch could flash around the cave and saw the water Mark had mentioned, and the wall above it, which cavers must use to traverse the area without getting wet. She didn't want to think what lay beyond that in the blackness, and found herself shivering when she thought about how deep into the earth they already were.

'OK, victim on the stretcher,' Mark ordered, and she realised the rescue team had already assembled the folding stretcher.

'We have to strap you to it rather firmly,' Mark told her apologetically as she lay down on the light-framed contraption.

'I'll strap her in. I've done a lot of helicopter rescues and know how important it is to have the patient strapped just right.'

'You're not even a member,' Ella reminded him in an angry whisper as he fitted a collar to her neck, working so close to her body it began to shiver, but not from trepidation this time.

'And you're a bloody fool to do this SES stuff,' he whispered right back, folding her arms across her chest, hands to opposite shoulders, then strapping them in place. 'The town needs a live doctor, not a dead bloody heroine. Why can't you accept that you don't need to prove anything to these people?'

He didn't wait for an answer but turned to Mark.

'What kind of injuries does she have?'

'Let's give her a broken leg,' Mark said cheerfully, and Nash grumbled they should have thought of that first and treated it before they'd strapped her to the stretcher. But he went ahead, getting one of the other volunteers to splint the leg properly then stabilise it on the stretcher.

Then he finished tightening the straps, pausing momentarily to touch Ella on the cheek.

'Not too tight?' he said, but his voice was anxious and Ella, getting more nervous by the moment, heard it as an endearment and tucked it away in her heart to consider later.

She lay still as the stretcher was tied to ropes and hauled up to the crawl space.

'I'll be right behind you,' Nash said as the rest of the team crawled ahead, needing to get through before they could pull the stretcher on its perilous journey. And he was, touching her leg every now and then as if he guessed how scary it was to be lying helpless on her back, looking up at a stone ceiling only inches above her nose, hauled along like a package, over rocks and stones, and around bends that seemed impossible to negotiate.

Then finally they were in the big tube and men were carrying the stretcher so Ella's ride was easier. Until they came to the boulder choke, and once again she had to be hauled over the rocks and through a narrow aperture.

'One more lift and you're done,' Mark said to Ella, peering down at her as she lay on the floor of the top tube, right under the access hole. 'Bob wants us to do a double lift, just to make sure the crew can manage it. We've decided Nash is the heaviest and he'll balance you, being the lightweight.'

Suspicions that Nash had had more than a few quiet words with his old friend swirled in Ella's head, but right now she was more concerned with how the lift would be done.

She soon found out as she was unstrapped from the stretcher, though her leg remained in a splint so standing upright unaided was impossible.

She sat, stiff-legged on the ground, while two volunteers dismantled the stretcher and folded it into a neat bundle. Worrying about doing nothing, she tried again to stand, but the splint was too bulky.

'Stay still, I'll lift you,' Nash said, and she turned to see him hooked into a harness, a rope leading from it and up through the hole. But rather than lifting her, he sat down beside her.

'We just have to wait until the rest of the crew get topside so they can haul us out. Right now some of them are making heavy weather of climbing back up the rope.'

'Is that why you volunteered to be lifted out?'

'Not entirely,' he said, and though she'd turned out her headlamp she was sure he was smiling.

Someone yelled an order, and he stood up then bent over her, helping her to her feet, then clasping her against his body.

'I'm going to take your weight and I want you to put your good foot on my left foot. It's in a sling and it'll take the extra weight. If you were unconscious I'd strap you to me, but as you're not, just hold on tight.'

He wrapped a steel-hard arm around her and drew her closer, so close she was certain she could feel every muscle in his body.

'Hold on,' he said again, and, very reluctantly, she put her arms around his waist. 'And relax!'

It was an order, but one she couldn't obey. Tension contracted her muscles into hard, knotted lumps as she fought to resist the attraction of Nash's body.

'Isn't it fun?' he teased, as he positioned the two of them beneath their exit and gave the order for the team to pull them out.

No, it's not, Ella thought, but she didn't give him the satisfaction of an argument. She just clamped her lips shut and tried to pretend she was holding tightly to an electricity pole— No, that was a bad analogy—better not to think about electricity at all! Maybe she was holding onto a concrete pillar—like the ones that held the pier anchored to the sea-bed.

But her heart knew she was holding Nash, and her body was beginning to betray her as well, softening so it seemed to meld into his.

'Uh-oh, trouble! Hold still, you two.'

Whoever had called out didn't sound too concerned, but as the upward motion stopped and she and Nash were left dangling in the darkness, her body stiffened again.

'Hey, you'd just relaxed,' Nash reminded her, and the arm that held her close to him drew her even closer, then, in a manoeuvre she'd have thought impossible given their hard hats and lamps and the rope and their position, his lips found hers and he kissed her until the tension left her body, draining away but leaving a vacuum into which excitement stole.

'OK, guys, we're going again,' the same voice called, and Nash's lips left hers, though his body still provided warmth and comfort until they finally lifted free of the cave. Helping hands guided her away from Nash, laying her down on the ground because the exercise was not yet over and, as a patient, she needed to be readied for transport to a hospital.

Once satisfied the exercise was successfully completed and all equipment had been stowed away in the truck, Bob had everyone sit down on the soft grass of the headland and ran through a debriefing procedure, where members could offer suggestions of how the rescue could have been improved.

So it was late before they were dismissed, and Ella was intensely weary as she made her way to her car.

'Did you eat before all this excitement?' Nash asked, catching up with her and reminding her he'd driven so he had her car keys just before she had a panic about whether she'd lost them in the lava tubes.

She shook her head.

'Me neither!' he said, and she forbore from mentioning his grammar. 'Let's go to Shastri's.'

'Go to Shastri's? When I've crawled along tunnels and been dragged over boulders and through holes too small for a normal person to fit through? You've got to be joking!'

He laughed and put his arm around her shoulders, giving her a quick hug.

'You know I'd begun to think you weren't a normal woman. You know, not caring at all how you were dressed or what you looked like, but that comment was pure woman, Ella Marsden! You *do* care!'

He sounded delighted by his discovery but his words were like poison darts pricking Ella's skin.

Did she dress so badly that Nash had assumed that?

Had she lost all pride in her appearance?

She didn't think so, and although her wardrobe was limited and, yes, most of her clothes had reached the ancient stage, she still made sure she looked neat and tidy.

Depressed by where all this was leading, and hurt by his comments, she climbed into the passenger seat of her own car, rested her head against the headrest and swallowed hard.

Then she remembered the kiss and rustled up some anger to chase the sadness away. It was none of Nash McLaren's business how she looked.

He climbed in beside her and settled—smugly, she was sure—into the driver's seat.

'Do you kiss many abnormal women that you can judge

me as normal or not?' she demanded. 'And do they all have to be strapped to you so they can't escape your attentions?'

He turned towards her, and in the pale light reflected off the sea she could see his astonishment, then the glimmer of amusement that lit his eyes.

And in that instant she knew she'd gone too far.

'I don't think you tried hard to escape, Ella Marsden,' he murmured, then he hooked his hand behind her head, drew her close and kissed her again, only this time there was nothing comforting in the caress. It burned across Ella's lips with a heat that made her wince, and his tongue explored her mouth with an insistence that had her gasping, then his hand was on her breast, the bulky SES overall she still wore no protection from the flame that ripped through her as his thumb found her already peaked nipple and teased it into a frenzy of desire.

CHAPTER NINE

NASH felt her response and cursed the bulky overalls they both wore. Far too awkward to shed in the narrow confines of the car.

Whoa! What on earth was he thinking?

He drew back from the kiss and looked at the woman who'd led him this far astray. He was all but engaged to Karen.

He didn't know for sure, but he suspected the woman in his arms had already slept with his brother.

He was so damned confused his brain felt like it was on fire.

Maybe it was, which was why he was behaving this way.

Ella was watching him watching her, the dazed expression in her eyes changing to suspicion then to anger.

'All done kissing?' she asked, pushing him away and straightening in her seat. 'Remembered you had a girlfriend, did you? Or decided I was too badly dressed for even a brief holiday fling?'

'Oh, for heavens sake!' he muttered at her, turning the key in the ignition so fiercely the tired old vehicle coughed its objection and choked instead of starting. 'You were kissing me as much as I was kissing you, and you knew I had a girlfriend. And I didn't mean to insult you with that remark— it was just surprising to hear you go all girly about how you looked when I suggested dinner. We could have gone home and changed.'

He tried turning the key again, more gently, and this time the engine started.

'It's already after ten,' Ella pointed out, sitting back in her seat with her arms folded firmly across the full breasts he'd so recently touched. 'Shastri's closes at eleven. They'd hardly welcome people coming in at a quarter to, and what's more I did not go all girly on you, I just happened to mention I didn't want to dine out with lava tube mud all through my hair.'

She flicked a slightly muddy curl with her fingers as she spoke.

He had no answer—not to her accusations or to the way he felt, which was confused and excited and almost in love with the woman still fuming quietly in the seat beside him.

Almost in love?

How could his head have come up with that one?

Maybe his head hadn't—maybe his heart had.

And although the road was bumpy enough to need both hands on the wheel, he lifted one and slapped himself with the heel of his hand. Coming back to Edenvale had caused a regression of some kind. He was eighteen again and thinking with his pants, not his brain.

Absorbed in this silent chastisement, he failed to register the noise he heard as the scrap of Bach Karen had selected as the ring tone on his mobile, and it took a prompt from Ella—'Is that your phone?'—for him to recognise it.

He stopped the car and fished inside the overalls, wondering what would have happened if it had rung during the exercise. Would he have heard it in the caves?

It *had* been stupid to join in when it had meant both doctors had been unavailable. Stupid and unprofessional.

He'd intended staying with the group at the top, then hadn't been able to restrain himself, worrying about Ella's safety and needing to be near her in case his presence in some way could keep her safe.

'Nash McLaren,' he said, finally locating the phone and bringing it to his ear.

'Oh, Nash, it's Marg. Neville's just collapsed.'

Marg's voice was distorted, echoing.

'Is he breathing?'

'No, but he's got a pulse. I know CPR—we all do at the

surgery. I did five breaths then pressed the speed-dial for your number then five more breaths. I'm on speaker-phone and breathing for him between talking to you, but I don't know if I'm doing it right,' Marg whimpered.

'Whatever you're doing, it'll help,' Nash assured her. 'Ella's with me and we're on our way. I'll phone for the ambulance.'

He shut off the phone and passed it to Ella.

'You have a direct number for the ambulance? It's Neville Neal. They still live in Abalone Street?'

Ella, already keying in numbers, nodded, then spoke quickly but clearly to whoever answered. But she was swearing quietly under her breath as she disconnected.

'Trouble?'

'The ambulance is at a motorcycle rally further down the coast. The person on duty will phone triple 0 for a standby vehicle to be sent. If our lousy, lazy member of parliament doesn't get a second ambulance stationed here in the new year, I'll start rumours spreading about the affair he's been having with his secretary.'

'Is he having an affair with his secretary?' Nash asked, startled by the bitter anger in Ella's voice but intrigued by her threat.

'I don't know and I don't care. His secretary's a man, so that should make it even better, especially as Jason—that's the secretary—is the most obstructionist, vindictive opportunist spin-doctor in the world. You wait, within a couple of days I'll have started the meningococcal outbreak and his highness the local MP will have brought in the Health Department and saved the town!'

And in spite of his anxiety over Neville, whom he'd known since Marg had started work for his father twenty years ago, Nash found himself chuckling at Ella's wrath.

Glad also that he wasn't the cause of it for once.

'Is the town big enough for two ambulances?'

'Of course it is. And we could have two, and staff for them, but the ambulance station—the building itself—is old and outdated and needs rebuilding, and that's the priority. If I could get a new ambulance station built, then getting the second vehicle would be easy.'

Nash smiled to himself at the commitment in her voice. It was a wonder she wasn't building the station brick by brick herself. He turned into Abalone Street and pulled up in front of Marg's house. Ella leapt out and opened the back door, and only then he realised he hadn't asked her if she had a bag with her.

Of course she did. It hadn't taken long for him to realise just how efficient she was.

He went straight into the house, where he found Neville no longer unconscious but grey and sweaty and obviously ill.

'He's just thrown up,' Marg said, 'so I guess it's just a virus. Sorry I panicked you two.'

'Don't be sorry,' Ella said, holding Neville's wrist as she counted his pulse. 'And it might not be a virus.'

She studied Neville's face for a moment, then gave an infinitesimal shrug.

'Didn't you tell me you'd passed out once before?'

'You didn't tell me you'd passed out once before!' As Marg exploded into indignation, Nash understood Ella's shrug. She'd weighed up the situation and decided patient confidentiality no longer mattered. She must think there was something much more important at stake.

Neville was trying to calm his wife, explaining he hadn't wanted to worry her, but Marg refused to be comforted, announcing she was driving him to the city right now, where they'd stay with her mother and he'd have every test the specialists could think of until they found out what was wrong with him.

'I think that's a good idea,' Ella said to Marg, 'but let's send Neville in the ambulance just to be sure.'

She turned to Neville to explain. 'You'll be admitted to hospital and may need to stay in for a few days so they can monitor you. If it's a slight arrhythmia causing these turns, then a pacemaker, which is fitted in a very simple operation, will soon sort you out. You won't even know it's in there—except when you get to the security checkpoints at airports or in public buildings in the city, where you'll have to be manually searched and guided through another entry.'

'Manually searched by a pretty girl, I hope,' Neville joked, and Nash felt the tension drain out of the atmosphere as everyone relaxed.

They waited until the ambulance arrived and saw Neville off, Ella assuring Marg that Kate would be happy to work in her place until she was ready to return. But as they walked out to the car Nash asked the question that had been bugging him but that he hadn't wanted to ask in front of Marg and Neville.

'What if it's not a simple arrhythmia?'

Ella stopped walking so she could face him, and he could see the tiredness in her pale skin and drooping shoulders.

'Then the specialists will find whatever's causing the problems and fix it,' she said. 'But I didn't see any reason why the pair of them should have to worry all the way to the city and then through the next few days about whether or not Neville might need a valve replacement, or a multiple bypass, or any of the other things I could have mentioned.'

'You're good!' Even to him, the words sounded as if they'd been dragged reluctantly from his vocal cords.

And, of course, Ella picked up on it.

'Don't overwhelm me with praise,' she snapped, marching away from him and climbing into the car.

'I'm sorry, that came out wrong, but I meant it. I see it all the time, and hear it from the patients. You're good because you care about people. Not just about their illnesses but about their effect on them and their families. Even Mr Warburton grudgingly admitted you'd done some good things in the town—like setting up a support group for carers. He said his wife isn't nearly as anxious and fussy with him as she used to be, since she started going to the carers' meetings and listening to things you tell them.'

Which reminded him of something else he'd been meaning to say to her.

'Do you get any time for yourself? You rush home when you can in the afternoons to spend time with Brianna, which is natural, but with the SES and the carers' group and your talks at the high school, and another support group Josh was telling me about for families with children with special needs, do you ever have time just for yourself?'

He was standing by the car, holding the door open, peering in at where she'd strapped herself into the passenger seat. Naturally, the ancient ruin had no inside light, so her face was in shadow, but he could feel her tension, though he was at least two feet away.

'Shut the door and let's get home,' she said, and she sounded so tired he obeyed her.

He shut the door, walked around the back of the vehicle and got in himself, then drove home.

He pulled up where the car had been parked earlier, right next to the front steps of the house.

'I don't leave it here. I lock it in the garage at night. There's an alarm system down there and with both the car locked and the garages locked, I sleep better at night.'

'Well, you hop out here and I'll put the car away. You're exhausted.'

She was exhausted, but as she climbed out of the car and dragged herself up the steps to the veranda, she was also resentful. Resentful of the angry accusation in Nash's voice when he'd said it. OK, so he was probably tired as well, but he hadn't needed to come on the exercise, so if he was tired that was his problem and he shouldn't take it out on her.

She made her slow way through the house, not needing to be quiet with both Brianna and Mrs Carter away, straight to the shower to get rid of the dirt, dust and mud she'd picked up during the exercise. Hot water might also wash away some of her troubled thoughts.

Wrapped in a towel, she headed for her bedroom, opening the bottom drawer in the old dresser in search of something to wear to bed. Nash's 'girly' crack echoed in her head and she felt a pang of regret for the filmy, floaty night attire she saw in catalogues for luxury lingerie.

'Probably acutely uncomfortable,' she muttered to herself, grabbing an old green T-shirt one of her friends had given her back when six of them, five women and Rick, had shared a house. Back when they'd laughingly called themselves his harem. Back in what seemed like another life! The T-shirt was long enough to cover her decently, and of such soft, worn cotton it was bliss to sleep in. Then, knowing if she didn't eat something hunger would wake her in a couple of hours, she went through to the kitchen, poured a glass of milk, set it to warm for ten seconds in the microwave, then made herself a honey sandwich.

The footsteps startled her at first, then she remembered Nash was staying here. She held up her sandwich as he came in.

'Want a honey sandwich?'

'I'll fix myself something,' he said, but instead of moving to either the pantry or the fridge he settled in a chair across from her. 'I was out of order this evening,' he began. 'You were right—there was no way both of us should have been on that exercise. But perhaps while I'm here I can take your place on the SES team and you can do the calls on those nights.'

Ella was tired, but not so tired the offer didn't sound suspicious.

'Why?'

'To give you a break. It's strenuous work on top of your already heavy workload.'

'My workload is none of your business!' she snapped. 'And, no, you won't take my place on the team. The whole idea of practice and meetings is that the team works as a unit—you taking my place is going to disrupt the unit then you'll head off back to the city and I'll have to fit back into the team. You can be on call while I'm at meetings—that's why I wanted a locum at this time of the year when the SES is busiest.'

He scowled at her but that wasn't unusual so she ignored it and drank her milk, although her sandwich now tasted like very sweet cardboard and she knew she wouldn't finish it.

'Well, I'm going to bed,' she said, and was about to push back her chair when Nash reached across the table and caught her hand.

'It doesn't have to be like this, Ella,' he said quietly, 'with the two of us fighting all the time. We were friends once—couldn't we be friends again?'

To have a friend in Nash! It was second highest on her impossible dream list! And no prizes for guessing what was top!

But Nash had Karen, who hadn't looked like a woman who'd want her man to have female friends. Besides, being friends with Nash and nothing more would probably kill her—Ella, not Karen! No, number one and two on her impossible dream list had to go together—friends *and* lovers or nothing.

'No, I don't think so,' she said, and tried to stand up again, but his hand held her wrist against the table.

'Why not?' Steel grey, his eyes were tonight, and as hard as the metal they resembled.

'You're being stupid. It doesn't even need discussion. You're only here to spy on me, or try to talk your mother out of selling to me. Friends!' she scoffed. 'Friends do things together, enjoy seeing each other, share! Once you've got me out of here, I'll probably never see you again—and it'll be another five months, or more, before you visit your mother again.'

Remembering his neglect of his mother had helped fire her anger and she glared at him across the table.

And she'd obviously scored, for he rubbed his fingers through his hair and nodded slowly.

'I've been working weekends—more than weekends, often

seven-day weeks,' he said, and, seeing how tired he suddenly looked, she believed him.

'Why?'

He lifted his head to stare at her in disbelief.

'You ask why? Are you so cocooned from reality down here you haven't heard about the crisis in public hospitals—about the difficulty of getting quality staff to man A and E departments? I've worked because I've had to.'

She did know about staffing problems in public hospitals and knew about the lack of beds and all the other trouble, so why didn't she believe him?

'Seven-day weeks?' she repeated. 'Do you think a patient seeing a doctor who's worked heaven knows how many hours or days straight is getting quality service? It's nuts to be working like that, Nash McLaren, and, what's more, you've spent enough time in A and E to know it. Mistakes happen when doctors are overtired.'

'I don't make mistakes!'

The growl should have told her to shut up, but she'd remembered something she'd once read in a medical journal.

'Yet!' she said, then she studied him for a moment before offering her theory—a theory she knew was going to blow the lid right off his anger. 'Statistical evidence suggests that doctors who push themselves too hard, blaming pressure of work and a need to be there, are often escaping from something else in their lives. An unhappy home life or a bad relationship were two of the situations mentioned in the report I read.'

Streaks of red appeared on his cheekbones, and though his eyes weren't exactly shooting sparks, it was easy to imagine they could.

'My working life is none of your business,' he said, with what Ella realised was admirable restraint. 'But as you've brought up the subject of that study—which I also saw—doesn't it also apply to you? Isn't this what we were discussing back at Marg and Neville's place—your working hours and habit of throwing yourself into everything you possibly can? What are *you* escaping, Ella Marsden?'

She tilted her chin and glared at him, furious he'd turned the tables on her.

'I did my escaping years ago,' she said. 'Now I've come back and I'm rebuilding—rebuilding a real life with a solid base and with promise for the future.'

But knowing that at the moment her dream had turned shaky made her feel weak inside, and her anger died, replaced by despair.

'If you don't spoil it all!' she whispered, then she tried again to stand up—to escape before he saw the tears she was desperately trying to hold back.

But he must have seen them, for he was out of his chair and moving around the table, his hand still clasped like a handcuff to her wrist. So it was easy for him to haul her against his chest, where he released her wrist and wrapped both arms around her, murmuring nothing words into her still damp hair.

Too tired to understand what was happening, apart from the delight her body felt in Nash's arms, she slumped against him, then, as if it was the most natural thing in the world, she lifted her face for a kiss.

This was crazy. They hated each other. Well, maybe not hated exactly, but certainly distrusted.

Then the kiss blotted out all thought. The feel of Nash's lips on hers, the slow burn of desire through her body, the little cry, half moan, half plea, as his hand cupped her breast and his thumb once again brushed across her pebbling nipple—her mind whirled to somewhere else, somewhere doubts and suspicion and worry were outlawed and happiness was being held in Nash's arms.

A few years later—though time must have stood still for the clock said only minutes had passed—Nash lifted his head and looked down into her eyes, his own hot with desire.

'We've unfinished business, Ella Marsden, and we both know it.'

He lifted one hand and ran the back of it down her cheek, his touch as light as the petals on the daisy crowns Sarah wove.

'But tonight's not the night. You're exhausted and I'm on call, and I'm damned if I'm getting up halfway through making love to you to go out and minister to a sick child. I'd probably kill the caller!'

He smiled, the kind of smile that made her heart falter and her mind forget he had a Karen, then he kissed her again, but gently this time, before turning her in his arms so she was pointing towards the door and saying, 'Go now, before it's too late.'

Was he mad?

Nash gave her a gentle shove in the direction of the door, while his body throbbed with wanting her and his mind screamed at such stupidity. He could have lifted her into his arms and carried her through to his bedroom, and she wouldn't have made a single protest.

Even now he could grab one of those still damp curls and haul her back to where she belonged—in his arms.

But she *was* exhausted, and he *was* on call. She deserved better.

He watched her move, as if in a dream, towards the door. Slow shuffling steps, but her lack of speed made it easier for him to admire the long naked legs below the hem of the disreputable green T-shirt she obviously wore as a nightdress.

His gaze moved from up the legs to a pert bottom and, just before she disappeared from view, lifted even higher.

To where the writing was!

Writing he couldn't help but read.

Writing that said, RICK MARTIN—SEX GOD.

He wanted to hit something but if he pummelled the table Ella would hear and come back to the kitchen and he'd probably hit her.

No, of course he wouldn't hit her, but he wouldn't mind hitting Rick Martin.

What rot! He'd never hit anyone in his life!

But now he was remembering Rick Martin's visit—and he doubted there were two Rick Martins Ella would hug—and how the man had looked at Ella, how she had looked at him.

Old friends, huh?

As if!

Yes, he'd certainly like to hit Rick Martin!

He was down by the beach and there was a big heart spray-painted on the outside wall of the old bathing pavilion with the words 'Ella loves Rick' on an arrow through the middle of it. He was eating something—Rick Martin's heart?—and it was giving him indigestion, so he had a pain in his chest.

Then music started up—an orchestra on the beach—and now Ella was there, trying to rub the heart off the wall. No, she was rubbing at a name—at Rick's name—and she had her own can of spraypaint so maybe she was going to spray another name in its place.

He was holding his sore stomach and trying to see how she was going when something about the music the orchestra was playing impinged on his consciousness.

He reached for the phone, knocked it off the bedside table to the floor, found the switch for the lamp and finally retrieved the still ringing mobile.

'Nash McLaren!' He scraped his fingers through his hair, rubbing hard at his scalp to wake himself up. He couldn't possibly have been going to say 'Rick Martin'!

Listened to a frantic mother...

'Yes, Mrs Wilson, I know the place. Give her two aspirin, if she can take them, and keep her cool. Sponge her down with wet cloths. I'm on my way.'

Dreams were forgotten as he scrambled into clothes, left the house, then jogged down the drive to the garages. How did Ella feel, doing this trek at night, knowing her sister had been killed by a drug addict—knowing someone might be lurking in the trees around the surgery?

They should build new garages closer to the house...

He knew he was only thinking that because he didn't want to think anything else—didn't want to think he might have been wrong in his diagnosis of Kylie's rash earlier in the week. According to Mrs Wilson, she now had a raging fever. Meningococcal and septicaemia went hand in hand. Young people died from septicaemia. Was Ella right—had be been working too hard to be effective as a doctor?

He unlocked the garage and drove his car out, heading swiftly through the town.

He didn't think so, but he knew she had been right in her suggestion that there might be a reason he'd been pushing himself so hard—a reason outside his work.

Don't think about it now—think septicaemia, he reminded himself, and he ran through the protocols he knew so well. Septicaemia he could treat on an isolated property, but if Kylie had gone into septic shock…

He slowed down, searching the side of the road for the old silver cream can Mrs Wilson had told him had been converted into a mailbox. His lights caught the gleam of silver just ahead, and he slowed further to turn in over the cattle grid.

'Let it not be meningococcal,' he muttered to himself, wondering if St Jude, the patron saint of hopeless causes, might happen to be listening. Though realistically it was a stupid prayer. If Kylie had septicaemia she was a very sick young woman and the results could be just as devastating. His prayer had been selfish—not for Kylie at all, but for himself in case he'd been wrong.

As he pulled up outside the old farmhouse, ablaze with light, he apologised to St Jude for bothering him.

He took one look at his patient and told Mr Wilson to phone for the ambulance, then set to work, examining Kylie gently, feeling the dry burning skin, hearing the rapid breathing, listening to her tachycardic heart. He started IV fluids and a broad-spectrum antibiotic, with an antipyretic to bring down the temperature, and told Mrs Wilson to keep sponging.

It was time to examine her more closely but, knowing with

a fever like she had she'd be sore all over, he'd have to be careful.

'Has she complained of pain—or a sick stomach?' he asked Mrs Wilson.

'She's— It's that time of the month—she always gets cramps.'

Nash pressed his hand gently on the girl's lower abdomen and felt her flinch even before she cried out with pain.

'Does she use tampons?' he asked, remembering a case study he'd read of a girl who'd died of septicaemia in a swimming pool, without being aware of how sick she had been.

Mrs Wilson nodded, and Mr Wilson returned from the phone at the same time.

'The ambulance's taken someone to the city,' he said. 'The switchboard said they'd get another one out here, but it could take hours.'

'What do you drive?' Nash asked him, though mentally he was remembering that the ambulance had taken Neville, and feeling Ella's anger that the town was so ill-equipped for emergencies.

'Big four-by-four!'

The reply was expected.

'Then we'll drive her,' Nash said. 'If you could put some pillows and blankets into the back seat and fill a cool box with ice so we can keep water cold for sponging her, then if one of you drive, I'll sit in the back with her to monitor her on the trip.'

'I'll drive,' Mr Wilson said. 'Jane will have to stay here for the littlies.'

He put his arm around his wife and gave her a hug.

'I'll look after her for you, love.'

'You go and get the car ready,' Nash said, not wanting to examine the girl further with her father in the room. More for his sake than for Kylie's.

He found a plastic bag, then explained to Kylie and her mother what he was going to do. Lifting the hem of her night-dress just far enough to see, and spreading her legs, he saw the tell-tale string of a tampon, but instead of being white the string was brown, and the stench as Nash gently withdrew it told him where the infection had started.

He sealed it in the bag, then in another one, then into a container and screwed down the lid so the infected object was contained until it could be disposed of properly.

Mrs Wilson left to put a bag of clothes and toiletries together for her daughter, while Nash put a pad between the girl's legs to absorb any discharge then let her mother slip panties onto Kylie to keep it in place.

A light beep of a car horn told him Mr Wilson was ready, and, once again explaining what he was about to do to the almost comatose girl, he picked her up and carried her in his arms out to the car.

Makeshift medicine, that's what it was, he thought as Mr Wilson drove fast but carefully through the night. But with no ambulance available, if there'd been no doctor to come out, the girl he was tending could have died.

They reached City Hospital as dawn was breaking, and the staff on duty, alerted by his phone call as they'd driven through the suburbs, teased him about not being able to stay away from the place. But at the same time they were ultra-efficient, settling Kylie on a stretcher, attaching the near-empty bottle of fluid to a stand and wheeling her away, as cheerful as if they had been at the beginning not the end of a twelve-hour shift.

Taking Mr Wilson by the arm, Nash followed them, knowing his presence would ensure Kylie got prompt attention. And she did. A gynaecologist was called in immediately, specimens taken and rushed to the lab, and Nash's replacement head of A and E took a personal interest in the case.

Once satisfied all that could be done was being done, Nash took the weary and worried father to the canteen, where they ordered an early breakfast and, while they waited for it to be cooked, phoned Mrs Wilson to report.

'Good thing we're not still milking,' Mr Wilson said, when

he and Nash sat down to eat. 'Jane would have had to do it all on her own. Not that she wouldn't have managed—she's a great woman. Kylie's good, too.' His voice quavered a little but he took a deep breath and continued. 'Good in the house, helping Jane, and with the kids, but she was good on the farm, too. Loved the animals. Even though she's a girl, I'd have left the farm to her.'

'You're not milking any more?' Nash asked, remembering conversations with his mother and Ella about the decline in the dairy industry.

'Nah! I've sold up. Developers offered so much money— well, with three kids to feed and educate, it was hard to say no. But they don't want the place right now, so we can stay on in the house, sort of indefinitely, as long as I keep the grass and weeds down.'

He didn't seem too happy with this easing of his workload, a suspicion confirmed when he added, 'Don't know why I did it, really. Greed, I suppose. But I'm a bit lost now.'

'You in the SES?' Nash asked.

His companion shook his head.

'Live too far out of town. I don't get to hear the siren, and even if I did, the truck'd be gone before I got to town.'

'You could do managerial-type of work for them,' Nash suggested. 'You must have kept books when you were dairying. You could do that kind of thing, and check equipment. You could be part of practice sessions even if you can't go out on jobs. And you'd know something about machinery— you could do research projects for them, looking at how other services run and the equipment they use. Bob Carruthers was telling me a lot of the equipment needs replacing but no one has time to look at the new things they're bringing out.'

'I could do that,' Mr Wilson said, looking happier than Nash had yet seen him. He just wished Ella had been there to see it—and to realise he, too, could do things to help the town.

Then he remembered what had been written on her T-shirt and had to bite back a growl.

CHAPTER TEN

ELLA woke late and shot out of bed, certain something must have happened to Brianna. Then, remembering Brianna was at Sarah's, she wandered through to the kitchen to fix herself a cup of tea. She'd take it back to bed and luxuriate in the delight of having a quiet morning all to herself.

As she walked back through the sitting room, automatically checking the answering-machine on her private phone—light flickering, message there—she glanced towards the other side of the house, wondering if Nash was awake, thinking of the kisses they'd exchanged and of the way they'd parted—he gruffly kind because she'd been tired, but between them promises for the future.

She smiled to herself, remembering the phrase he'd used.

Unfinished business!

And though she was aware that's all it was to him, she'd reached the stage where she'd accept whatever he offered. She knew that showed a total lack of pride—it was like a beggar accepting crumbs from the table of a rich man—but if crumbs of Nash were all she could have, at least they'd be crumbs she could hold in her heart for ever.

Along with the memory of her first kiss, and walks on the headland—kisses on the headland...

Telling herself how pathetic she was, she pressed the button on the answering-machine, and her heart did its blipping, flipping thing when she heard his voice.

Totally devoid of emotion, he was advising her he'd taken a patient, Kylie Wilson, suffering from septicaemia, up to town and he wouldn't be back until mid-afternoon at the earliest. He hoped she'd manage without him.

'I've managed without you for twelve years,' she told the

149

machine, snapping it off before the message repeated itself. Though why she was cross she didn't know!

Liar! Of course she knew! If he wasn't coming back till later, he'd be seeing Karen. Kissing *her* in the kitchen and probably taking Karen out to a spiffy, five-star restaurant.

She ground her teeth, took her cup of tea back into the kitchen and tipped it down the sink. Then she went back into her bedroom to change and whistled for the dogs. Perhaps she could walk off her bad mood before surgery began.

But as she walked, her mind cleared of her disappointment that Nash had stayed in the city. Now reality set in, and she admitted to herself she wasn't the kind of woman who'd have accepted Nash's crumbs—or, if she had, she'd have regretted it later. And hurt later…

So that was it. The Nash-Ella relationship—such as it had been—was over.

With that resolved, other problems she'd had little time to consider raised their beady little heads.

Chief among these was Brianna.

Exactly what were the implications if Brianna was Russell's child and therefore Sarah's grandchild?

Nash's niece, too, Ella realised, and that thought was truly frightening.

Nash and Sarah combined made two of them against one. Two McLarens who could claim some right to bring up the child who was now Ella's whole life.

She gave a snort of derisive laughter—Nash didn't know how right he'd been when he'd attacked the paucity of her life. But she had Brianna, and the joy Meg's daughter brought her was immeasurable.

The easiest thing to do was to ignore the whole resemblance issue—or put it down to environment and Brianna picking up some of Sarah's mannerisms.

But was that fair to Sarah, who'd been so good to both of them?

Of course it wasn't!

But Ella felt physically sick, considering what tests might

prove, and, worse still, the consequences of those tests. Maybe she could talk to Nash about it. But thinking about Nash made her think about the way he'd held her last night—as if she was something very precious. Too bad if Karen was lunching with him at a five-star restaurant. Last night's embrace had been a promise and if Nash wanted a brief affair with *her* while he was in Edenvale, and if Karen didn't know about it and she wouldn't, then, really, the only person who'd be hurt would be herself when he left. But she'd be prepared for that, and would handle it.

'I am totally nuts!' she said to Jobba and Priest, who were walking sedately beside her, while Harry, missing Brianna, was running back and forth in front of them, nose to the ground, pretending he was a bloodhound. 'In twenty minutes I've convinced myself I don't want an affair with him, and now I'm back convincing myself it would be OK. What's worse, I'm considering an affair with a man who would be cheating on another woman. I've got to get to work—do something that might get my brain working properly again. Do something to put Nash McLaren right out of my mind!'

She strode back home, had a quick breakfast, dressed for work, although it was two hours before she needed to be there, pulled Meg's briefcase with its precious notes out from under her bed and headed down to the surgery. She could spread the papers out across her desk and get stuck into the figures. This resolution reminded her that maths wasn't her best subject, which brought Nash right back into the forefront of her mind, but she shook him away. Two weeks to Christmas and she really, really wanted the money paid before then so the new year would be new in every way.

Once again other thoughts intruded—her plan had been for the start of the coming year to be the beginning of her new life as well, a permanent life in Edenvale. Bloody Nash McLaren butting in again!

She pushed him out of her thoughts again, and sat resolutely at her desk. She already had a list of the co-op's shareholders at the time it had folded, and the number of shares they'd held, but nowhere in her research had she found exactly how much money had been lost, or how that had impacted on the various shareholders. She was hoping the final annual report—the one she'd been photocopying when Nash walked into the library—would have that information.

By the time she heard Kate's key in the outside door, she'd found some of what she needed—the gross total—but still had to work out the percentages of that figure based on the number of shares held by each individual. Then figure out the little matter of twelve years' interest…

She sighed and shoved the papers roughly together. Maybe this afternoon she'd get it finished.

Bob Carruthers was her first patient, grumbling because Nash wasn't there and he'd have to be seen by a woman.

'You don't treat me like a woman at SES training,' she reminded him, 'so don't think of me that way now. What's up?'

'I've hurt my shoulder. Must have done it at the training last night. Doesn't feel like a muscle but the damn thing's as sore as blazes. I can hardly lift my arm.'

Ella sat him down, and took off his shirt, then didn't have to move his arm or shoulder to see the problem.

'Where's Merrilee? You guys not talking that you didn't ask her to take a look?'

Ella knew she was on safe ground, teasing him like this. Two more besotted people than the Carruthers she had yet to meet, in spite of six years' marriage and four kids under five.

'She's taken the kids up to her parents' place on the mid-north coast. I'm joining them for Christmas. What is it?'

'It's an abscess,' Ella told him, feeling gently around the hot, red, swollen site. There was no obvious pus and no core she could feel so she added, 'Or I'm guessing it is, although it could be a bite, or a tick that's burrowed in under the skin.'

'I'm allergic to ticks, but usually when they bite me I get a bit of asthma, not a sore arm.'

Ella found her magnifying loupe but even with that on, she couldn't see the black mark that would indicate a buried in-

sect or any puncture wounds to suggest a bite. Like Bob had
earlier, she now wished Nash were here. Maybe it was something he'd seen in A and E.

'How bad is the pain? Is it getting worse? Radiating from
the shoulder?'

'It only hurts when I move my arm,' Bob told her, 'or when
I bump against my back—like when I was putting on my
shirt, it hurt. And, no, I noticed it was really sore when I
rolled over in bed this morning, but I don't think it's any
worse.'

'I'll give you a painkiller and an antihistamine, but I'd like
you to stay here in one of the treatment rooms—or you can
sit in the waiting room—for a couple of hours just in case it
turns into something sinister.'

'Gee, thanks,' Bob said, but he seemed happy enough to
stay, opting for the waiting room.

Ella worked her way through the rest of the Saturday morning patients, glad it was mostly routine stuff—a case of flu
that had come on suddenly, and which she hoped wasn't the
start of a summer flu epidemic, a child with a cut foot, a
young man with gravel rash the length of his right arm and
leg from where he'd come off his trail bike onto a bitumen
road.

'I thought you were supposed to ride those bikes in the
bush, not on paved roads,' she chided as she gently removed
debris from his weeping wounds.

'I was riding up to where the bush track starts,' he told
her, but she knew some of the teenagers raced on a straight
stretch of road just out of town.

'Well, you won't be riding anywhere for a while,' she
warned him. 'And when you do get back on that bike, wear
protective clothing. Jeans and a long-sleeved shirt of some
thick material.'

She finished with him and saw him out then turned to Bob,
intending to take him into a treatment room for further ex-
ploration of his problem. But before she could speak to him

the door opened and Nash walked in, his face resembling the blackest of black stormclouds.

He greeted Bob civilly enough but scowled at Ella. Just as well she'd decided not to have that affair with him since he'd obviously gone off the idea! So much for unfinished business!

'I'm glad you're here,' she said, echoing words she was sure she'd said the previous Saturday. 'You can take a look at Bob's problem. Maybe you've seen something like this before.'

She led Bob through to the treatment room, and helped him off with his shirt, then sat him in a chair where she could shine a strong light on the swollen area.

Nash poked and prodded, obviously less gently than she had, for Bob protested loudly.

'You didn't think to open it up?' he said to Ella, icily professional yet with a touch of patronage in his tone.

'Where?' she snapped. 'There's no obvious infection site, there's no sign of something under the skin—do I cut at random then he has to get over the stitches as well as whatever's causing the problem?'

Bob ducked in his seat.

'I'm probably in more danger from the darts flying between you two than from whatever's happened to my shoulder. I thought, last night, you might be getting it together.'

'When hell freezes over!' Nash said, feeling under Bob's arm for signs of a swollen lymph gland.

But Ella was as puzzled over Nash's behaviour as Bob was. More so, in fact, given how they'd parted. OK, so *she'd* decided not to take their attraction any further, but Nash didn't know that.

She watched him go over all she'd done in her primary examination of Bob's shoulder, but knew from his face he was just as stumped as she was. If she hadn't been worried about her patient, she'd have been pleased.

'What treatment have you given him?' Icy grey eyes scanned swiftly across her face then settled on a point somewhere beyond her.

'Pain relief and an antihistamine injection. That was two hours ago and the swelling seems less hot now, but it hasn't changed to any noticeable degree.'

'Antibiotic?'

'If I could see infection, yes, but this?'

She waved her hand irresolutely in the air and to her surprise Nash didn't argue. In fact, he nodded.

'Let's give the antihistamine more time,' he suggested, but his eyes, as they rested on his old friend's back, were worried. 'Look, mate, how about you go home and rest? I know that sounds pathetic, but it's the best thing to do. If you feel at all sick, or if the pain gets worse, phone immediately. I'll be at the house all afternoon, or on my mobile, where Ella can reach me, if I go out.'

Taking over my patient! Ella thought, but she didn't say anything, knowing Bob would be happier dealing with Nash, and that Nash, with his contacts in A and E, could probably find out more about possible causes than she could.

Nash walked out with Bob, and when he didn't return, Ella locked up and walked up the drive to the house. She'd promised Brianna they'd make more Christmas decorations that afternoon, then while the little girl had her afternoon rest, Ella could get back onto the co-op figures. If she could get them out of the way this weekend, she might begin to feel the joy of Christmas.

With thundercloud Nash in the house?

Some hope!

Could it be an infection in a muscle or tendon? Nash wondered, lying on his bed, looking up at the ceiling, hearing Brianna's excited voice somewhere in the house and sometimes the softer murmur he knew must be Ella speaking to her daughter.

That was another puzzle—and one he'd better solve before too long. If Brianna was his mother's grandchild, then his mother deserved to know. Would he have to shake the truth out of Ella?

No, he'd think about Bob's shoulder, not shaking Ella, because, for one, he wasn't a violent man for all the violent fantasies he'd been having lately, and, for two, touching Ella was dangerous…

If a tendon was infected…

He must have drifted off to sleep, for next thing he was aware of was the silence in the house. Not total silence. Someone, Mrs Carter no doubt, was clattering pots together in the kitchen.

He got up and wandered in that direction, refusing a cup of coffee because he'd had another idea about Bob's shoulder while he'd slept.

'Does Ella keep medical books somewhere in the house?' he asked Mrs Carter.

She shook her head.

'She's got them all down in the surgery. Mostly in her office, I would think.'

Nash thanked her and left the house, telling himself it wasn't just an excuse to see Ella—in fact, the less he saw of her the better. Besides, she was probably off somewhere with Brianna, not down at the surgery at all.

But thinking of seeing her had reminded him of that morning when, standing close to her while they'd examined Bob's mystery swelling had been so difficult his skin had hurt.

He had to keep his distance, mentally and physically.

The thought made him laugh. That morning, when he'd called in to see Karen, determined to break up with her in person, not over the phone, she'd accused him of being in love with Ella—accused him of already sleeping with her. But it hadn't been Ella who'd brought him to his senses about his relationship with Karen—or if it had been, it had been her words about looking at his life, not his newly re-emerged attraction to her!

He was thinking that as he unlocked the surgery, locked the door behind him and headed for her consulting room, pushing open the door and walking in before he realised the room was already occupied.

She wasn't out with Brianna after all!

He saw Ella at about the same time as she screamed, then she realised who it was and stared at him in horror as she scooped papers off her desk, dumping them in an untidy heap beside it, smacking her hand on a calculator to turn it off and looking so guilty, all his suspicions about her presence in Edenvale came roaring back to life.

'What are you doing?' he demanded, aware his voice was far too loud.

'Figures. Paperwork.'

The words were lame and she knew it because her cheeks were a tell-tale scarlet.

'Oh, yes? Perhaps I can help? As I remember, you were never very good at maths.' He hadn't thought it possible for her to face to get redder, but it did, although he suspected an escalating anger was now adding to the molten heat in Ella's cheeks.

'Thank you, but I'd prefer to manage on my own,' she said, pretending to a coolness her cheeks belied.

He wasn't often prompted by the devil, but who else could have made him move forward, the offer as smooth as silk on his lips.

'Oh, no, let me help.'

Which was when she erupted with all the force of a pint-sized Vesuvius.

'Get out of here!'

Nash could feel the sparks of fury shooting off her, and if he hadn't been disturbed by the paperwork she'd swept aside, and still smarting over the T-shirt, he'd have laughed and taken her in his arms and kissed her anger away.

What *was* he thinking?

The only possible way he could get through the next three weeks was by keeping Ella Marsden at arm's length, and if he had to keep remembering she was a scheming, sexually irresponsible bitch to do it, then so be it.

But looking at the blazing fury, telling him some home truths about knocking before entering and keeping his nose out of other people's business, he knew he didn't really believe all those things, though he did believe there had to be something between her and Rick Martin and that was enough to make his own anger gnaw again at his stomach.

'I didn't know you were here. I came in to look up some medical texts. I was wondering if Bob's problem might be an infection in a tendon or muscle.'

He saw her shoulders slump as the anger drained away, and she sat back in her chair and waved her hand towards a small table by the window.

'Feel free. I've checked those books on the table and can't find any relevant information. I did read somewhere, in one of the recent AMA journals, I think, about underlying joint infection, though I doubt it could be that because the pain came on so suddenly. I've phoned the poisons centre, although I knew it wouldn't be a deadly spider—he'd be far sicker—and one suggestion was a red-back spider bite. A small red-back wouldn't leave much of a mark, and the pain and swelling seems symptomatic. Antihistamine and painkillers are the recommended treatment, but I did phone Bob and suggest he check his house in case Mummy and Daddy spider are somewhere about.'

Nash stared at her, wishing she didn't do this to him, wishing she wasn't so darned good at her job he kept feeling admiration for her.

Wishing also he didn't get a thrill from listening to her talk practical medicine. Things like Bob checking out his house for more spiders. That was what he'd always wanted—he remembered that now. He'd just been distracted by city life and the adrenalin rush of A and E, but now...

But now, if he came back he'd be kicking Ella out of Edenvale—doing exactly what she suspected he'd come back to do.

Although the town needed two doctors...

'We should get married!'

He wasn't sure where the words had come from. The voice

had certainly sounded like his, but it wasn't exactly the most thought-out statement of his life.

'Have you been drinking?' Ella demanded. 'Or just gone stark, raving mad? You come back here scowling and glaring at me, behaving so badly even Bob was aware of it, then you rip into me about Bob's treatment, and now you're suggesting marriage. And just where does Karen fit into this?'

'I broke up with Karen this morning.'

'Just so you could propose marriage to me?' Silky sarcasm slid through the words. 'Isn't that taking the saying about out with the old and in with the new just a smidgen too far?'

She lifted the phone and Nash panicked.

'You're not calling the police?'

Ella had to laugh. Her stomach was squirming, her mind was in chaos, and here she was, laughing.

'I'm phoning Josh. He's second in command at SES. It just hit me that perhaps the spider was in Bob's overalls last night.'

She'd got that far in her explanation when Josh answered, and she quickly told him what had happened.

'I was wondering how long it had been since the head-quarters were sprayed for pests. It might be a good idea to get onto it, or at least to get someone to check all the uniforms and helmets and the other gear.'

'Leave it with me,' Josh told her, 'and I'll go by and check on Bob, too. Maybe spend a couple of hours with him—we can have a game of cards.'

'Thanks, Josh.'

Ella hung up, passed on the message that Josh would check on Bob, then looked at her intruder, who was now slumped in a chair across her desk.

He was gaunt and unshaven and there were dark circles under his eyes. His hair was rumpled and his shirt looked as if he'd slept in it, which he probably had, but he'd never looked more appealing.

Don't go there, Ella's head warned, so she raised an eyebrow and waited for an explanation.

'I was thinking about the practice—thinking I'd like to stay, that I could really feel useful here and I like the patient contact and the involvement. Then I thought of Brianna, and if you don't want to admit to Mum about you and Russell then if we got married I could adopt her and she'd be Mum's grandchild—'

'Stop right there!' Ella said, holding up her hand. 'Admit *what* to Sarah about me and Russell? What me and Russell? You, of all people, should know that Russell had eyes for one woman and one only, and that was Meg.'

'But you look like Meg and he was so unstable and you're kind and you might have comforted him.'

Ella could feel the volcanic wrath she'd felt earlier rising again and, unable to control it sitting down, she rose to her feet and paced towards him so she could glare down at him.

'So you're suggesting I might have gone to bed with Russell out of pity? Knowing his illness? Knowing how close to the edge he often was? Would that be medical pity? A kind of treatment?'

She shook her head and moved away

'I can't believe I let you kiss me.'

'You didn't *let* me kiss you—you kissed right back. It was mutual!'

Nash was looking hurt, and most uncomfortable, a condition she understood when he added, 'And I didn't really think you'd sleep with Russell, but the resemblance is there and it was driving me crazy and I thought—'

'I know precisely what you thought.' Ella hoped the icy control she was trying to display was getting through, because inside she was a muddled mess, a little bit of her skipping up and down and suggesting she say yes to Nash's absurd proposal, while the rest of her wanted to kill him. 'You explained it quite succinctly. For your information, since you pointed it out, I've also been wondering about the resemblance, and wondering if Russell was Brianna's father—'

'There!' he said, standing up and moving so he was looming over her. 'You've admitted he might have been—now what's your excuse? Did you have so many men around at that time you weren't sure? Or was it just the sex god and Russell?'

Ella sank back down in her chair and waved a hand towards his, hoping he'd get the message and return to it. She rubbed her hands across her face and took a deep breath, then launched into an explanation that should have been made some time ago. A simple explanation!

One sentence!

'Nash, Brianna is Meg's child, not mine.'

'She's Meg's child?'

Ella nodded.

'Meg's daughter?'

Ella nodded again.

'Did Meg know who the father was?'

A nod was not enough this time.

'I assume so,' Ella told him, aiming for haughty this time, but, having caught his 'sex god' dig, she was so hot it was a wonder there wasn't smoke coming out of her ears. 'Because, contrary to your beliefs, Nash McLaren, the Marsden twins were not wild and neither were we promiscuous. I had been engaged to my fiancé for exactly two weeks and had had sex with him exactly once when Meg died and Brianna came into my life and he decided children didn't fit his lifestyle. We parted friends—probably with relief on his part as I wasn't very good in bed and he hadn't been very good with a twenty-six-year-old virgin. I don't have as precise details of Meg's sex life to offer you, but I'm reasonably sure she was as celibate as I was. Having a mother who ran off with a surfie ten years her junior but not before she'd entertained him in our house numerous times kind of puts you off sexual activity.'

Nash looked shell-shocked, as well he might. People did when they learnt about Ella's sex life—or lack of one. But the question, when it came, wasn't about that, but about Brianna.

'Didn't Meg tell you who the father was?'

The sadness she always felt over Meg's untimely death stole the heat from the fire within and she shook her head.

'Meg didn't think she'd die.' She offered the words carefully, aware that talking of Meg's death still had the power to shatter her control. 'What twenty-six-year-old does? She always said she would tell me one day, but that day didn't come.'

Ella sniffed and swiped a betraying tear from her cheek.

'Since you mentioned the resemblance to Sarah, though, I've been thinking maybe it was Russell. Meg was determined to come back to Edenvale, she wanted it far more than I did. I can't help wondering if it might have been so Brianna could grow up near her grandmother.'

Nash was scowling at her again, but her heart was too full of sadness now to care about Nash's scowls.

'I'd like you to go now, please, Nash,' she said. 'I've work to do.'

He scowled some more, opened his mouth to say something, shut it again and stood up.

'This conversation isn't finished!' he said, stomping out of the room but catching the door just short of a slam.

Ella put her head down on the desk and wept, but once the storm had passed and the excess emotion had been swept away in the flood of tears she straightened, wiped her eyes and face and hauled the pile of papers back onto the desk.

Nash marched up the drive, only vaguely aware that the weather had changed from sunshine to looming thunderclouds. It suited his mood exactly as he tried to assimilate too much information and too many reactions all at once.

Brianna was Meg's daughter. Weird relief.

Ella's fiancé had dumped her because she had chosen to look after the child. Anger mixed with weird relief.

Brianna might be Russell's daughter—boy, that one made him sad and happy at the same time.

His mother's granddaughter! He smiled at that.

His niece? Weird again.

He reached the turn and saw the house—saw his mother coming down the steps, anxiety etched in her face.

'Nash, thank God! It's Brianna. She's missing!'

CHAPTER ELEVEN

'BRIANNA and Pete. Josh dropped him over to play in the garden only half an hour ago and the phone rang and by the time I got back from answering it, they'd gone. Mrs Carter has searched the house and I was on my way down to the surgery to tell Ella.'

'I'll tell her,' Nash said, turning and sprinting back towards the surgery, overly aware now of the menacing weather. The thought of two children lost in a thunderstorm was terrifying! Bother the weather. What about Ella? He cursed the fact he'd upset her so much that she was already emotionally fragile.

This news would devastate her.

Wrong again.

'Well, they can't have gone far!' Ella declared, all businesslike common sense, but the colour that drained out of her face belied her composure, and Nash could see the pulse beating frantically in her temple as she willed herself to stay calm. 'Is Sarah sure they're not hiding somewhere? Have they searched the house and gardens? Yes, I suppose they have…'

Nash took her hand and held it tightly, explaining what had already been done, seeing the panic in her eyes, though she fought it with practicality.

'Is Harry with them?'

'The dog? I didn't think to ask.'

'Harry will look after her,' Ella said, and although she sounded positive he could see the white knuckles on her clenched hands and hear the crackling strain in her voice.

'We'll search the grounds before we call the SES.'

She was fumbling with the lock on the surgery door and he took the key from her shaking fingers and locked it himself.

'Garages first, then we'll work our way up each side of the drive.'

Nash shook his head, unable to believe she could think so clearly when the life of the person most dear to her might be at risk. Then he guessed she had to do this—had to stay calm—because the children needed help, not hysteria.

She led the way, calling to Brianna, whistling for the dogs. Priest and Jobba arrived and with them Girlie.

'Find Harry,' she said to them, but all three dogs just wagged their tails, delighted their adored Ella was talking to them.

Twenty minutes later they knew the two children weren't in either of the houses or the garden. Ella phoned Josh at Bob's place.

'The caves,' Josh said immediately. 'It's my fault. I was telling Pete about the rescue exercise.'

'And Brianna's been cave-mad lately, even getting a book out of the library. But they've never walked as far as the tourist caves.' Ella tried to put the panic to one side so she could think, while outside the rumble of thunder seemed to echo the dread in her heart.

'What about the headland?' Josh suggested.

'The headland where we went down?' Ella thought for a moment, then muttered, 'Damn! You could be right. You can see the caves from our headland—see the white fence around them.'

Her heart thudded so hard she had to press her hand against it. It was only a six-foot drop down the hole but a child could be badly injured in such a fall.

Nash took the phone from her now nerveless hand and spoke to Josh.

'OK,' he said, when he'd replaced the receiver. 'You and I will walk across to the headland—we'll take our mobiles so we can contact Josh. Bob says he's well enough to organise things so he'll deploy half the available men to search from our gate back towards town and send the rest to the headland.'

He'd have liked to tell Ella to stay at home but knew he'd

have no hope of persuading her not to be part of the search. And suddenly he understood just how much Meg's child, her only link with her adored twin and her sole remaining relative, must mean to her. As much or more than a child she'd borne herself.

'Come on.'

He explained to his mother where they were going, took the heavy waterproof coats she offered because the rain was getting closer and suggested she and Mrs Carter make sandwiches in case the search had to be widened and more volunteers brought in. At least the activity would divert some of their worries, though the pain and anxiety on both their faces told its own tale.

'I'll take Girlie,' Ella said. 'She's closest to Brianna and Harry.'

She called the dog who, happy to be going for a walk, loped along in front, returning every now and then to Ella's side.

'Where's Harry?' Ella asked her, and the intelligent dog looked at Ella then looked around.

'Find Harry,' Ella told her, and Girlie barked.

No answering bark, though they were down on the flat between the two headlands and the noise should have carried.

They climbed towards the top of the second one—the headland formed by the maze of lava tubes beneath it.

'Where's Harry?' Ella asked the dog again, and this time, when Girlie barked, they heard, or thought they heard, a faint echo of the noise.

'It could just be an echo,' Nash said, not wanting Ella to get too excited, but she was already running towards the fenced-off hole and peering down through the grate that was intended to stop adventurous tourists entering the lava tubes.

'The men put it back in place on Friday night,' Nash reminded Ella as she opened the gate and knelt by the hole. 'And the padlock's in place so you can see it hasn't been moved.'

But she ignored him, leaning low and calling to Brianna, Josh and Harry.

It was Harry who answered, his deep bark echoing up through the tubes, mimicking the thunder rolling overhead.

'Brianna, are you there, sweetheart? Is Pete with you? Are you all right?'

No answer, though Harry kept on barking.

'How—?' Nash began, but Ella was already sliding her legs between the bars.

'They're so wide apart I can get between them, so it would have been easy for the littlies to drop down. Phone Josh and get the whole crew here. Take my mobile and press four, and you'll get through.'

'You can't go down there without equipment,' Nash told her as she wriggled more of her body through the narrow aperture between the bars.

'The children might be hurt. If they dropped from here, they could both be unconscious.'

'And you'll land right on top of their unconscious bodies and make things worse.'

Josh answered the phone and as Nash explained, Ella said, 'I don't think they're underneath because Harry's bark is further away and he wouldn't leave them. I'll swing on the bar and jump wide—I had plenty of time to look around on Friday night and know where there's a pile of sand to the landward side of the hole.'

She wriggled through further, intending to hold the bars with her hands and swing before she dropped, but then Nash was off the phone, gripping her hands.

'I can lower you further. You won't have so far to drop, but don't go far into the system on your own, Ella. We don't want men risking their lives looking for three of you.'

'Four,' she said, as Nash lowered her down. 'There's Harry, too.'

The children weren't lying in an unconscious heap beneath the hole, but the explanation was. A rope ladder Ella knew belonged on Pete's cubby house was lying on the sand. He had fixed it to the bars, but as they'd both climbed down his knots had come undone, leaving them no way to get back up.

She explained this theory to Nash, who pointed out a dog couldn't climb down a rope ladder.

'You don't know Harry,' she said, and found a smile, remembering how the pair had taught Harry to get in and out of the cubby. But it had probably been Harry's weight that had brought it down—so Harry was both their saviour with the bark but the cause of their distress now.

'Brianna? Pete? Are you there, darlings?'

Ella called softly, partly because the echoes in the tubes could be frightening but also because the pair would already know they were in trouble and she didn't want them not answering to avoid it.

But there was no reply, although Harry's bark suggested they'd gone towards the boulder choke, no doubt looking for a way out.

'Don't go anywhere on your own—you've no light, no helmet.'

That was Nash giving orders from above, but it wasn't his beloved child who was missing. Besides which, the tube was well lit from the hole, though doubtless that light would disappear once she crawled through the space at the top of the rubble.

She whistled for Harry, thinking he might come and lead her back to the children, but though he barked—he was definitely on the other side of the boulders—he didn't come.

Ella called to Nash to tell him where she was going and though he cursed and forbade her to move, she knew she had to do it. But crawling through the narrow space with no light and no companions was scary and she prayed she'd made the right decision.

'Brianna,' she called again when she reached the other side and stared down into the darkness of the larger tube.

'Brianna's hurt her leg and so has Harry.'

Pete's small voice brought joy surging through Ella's heart.

'Can Brianna talk to you, Pete?' she asked.

'Sometimes,' Pete replied, and Ella guessed at concussion, then images of all the terrible things that could accompany a head injury rose up in her mind. But there was nothing she could do without light—and no way she could get down to where the children were without a rope.

'Pete, darling, I'm going to crawl back and get a light and some rope and I'll come back very, very soon and get you all out of there. You hold Brianna's hand and put your arm around Harry so you're all close together, and I'll be back very soon.'

There was a noise she didn't recognise echoing through the caves and by the time she'd crawled back over the rubble she guessed what it was. The cave was now entirely dark, lit only when a flash of lightning sneaked through some cover Nash had put across the grate. The noise was thunder and the sound of rain belting down on the ground and echoing through the tubes.

'Nash!'

She heard the quaver in her voice as she called his name, and relief shot through her body when he answered.

'I'm here, Ella, love,' he said. 'But I've put the spare coat over the grate to try to stop rain getting in. It's pouring down out here, but I can see the lights of the truck approaching. They'll be here in a couple of minutes. Did you find the children?'

He'd called her 'love'.

It was to keep her calm.

But it had sounded as if he'd meant it.

'Brianna's hurt!' she whispered, realising, as the pathetic sound came out, that she'd lost the control that had kept her going up till then.

'How badly?'

'I don't know!' She was weeping now and desperate. 'They're the other side of the boulder choke and I couldn't get down to them without a ladder— Oh, wait, Pete's cubby-house ladder is here. I'll take it back.'

'You stay right there,' Nash roared. 'Do not move a muscle, do you hear me? The truck's pulled up, there'll be properly equipped men down there within minutes, and as soon as they get down there, you're coming up.'

'But Brianna—'

'I'll get Brianna out. Do you think I don't care? You're too close to be detached, Ella, and you said yourself it was irresponsible for the town's two doctors to be down there at once.'

Ella knew he was talking sense, but if he thought she'd leave this cave before she had Brianna in her arms, he didn't know her very well.

Suddenly the tube was flooded with light and she could hear the roar of the generator that provided power for the SES's blindingly bright halogen lamps. She heard the grate being opened and was warned to stand clear. While Bob's voice was giving orders to erect a cover over the hole, a rope ladder was already slithering down.

It was no surprise to find it was Josh who came down first.

'Pete?' he asked, and Ella hugged him.

'Pete's OK. He's minding Brianna and Harry. He's a brave little boy.'

'He's too wild by far and I'll kill him,' Josh said, but Ella had felt the relief in his body and knew Pete would be hugged and kissed before a word of censure was uttered.

'Nash says you're to go back up and wait,' Josh said, then he grinned at her, handed her a helmet with a light and the small first-aid kit she could strap on her back.

'Thanks,' Ella said. 'Have you got another ladder? We'll need it to get to the lower level below the choke. That's where the kids are.'

He indicated he had the rolled ladder and also a small folded stretcher, but his mind was leaping ahead.

'They're in the tube that has the water in it? Damn! We've got to hurry, Ella. That cave fills up if we get a shower, let alone a deluge like we're getting topside at the moment.'

More dread to squeeze Ella's heart. She led the way towards the choke and crawled across, talking all the time to the children, telling Pete his dad was right behind her, talking although she knew they probably couldn't hear because already the sound of rushing water was echoing through the tubes.

Josh was right behind her, telling the other volunteers to wait where they were, as more people coming through the narrow tunnel would hinder the return.

'You OK, Pete?' she called when she reached the end of the crawl space.

'Yes, Ella, but it's getting wet in here.' Pete's voice was thin with fear.

'We'll have you out in no time. Your dad's fixing the ladder so we can come down and carry you up.'

She went first, shining her light so she could see where Brianna lay like a crumpled doll, Pete sitting beside her, his hand in hers, his face chalk-white in the yellow light.

'Thanks, Pete,' Ella whispered, swallowing hard as she knelt to examine the little girl. Harry, lying beside Brianna, whimpered so she thanked him, too, but one look at the angle of Brianna's leg told her all she needed to know about that injury.

So it was straight into ABCs. Airway—clear; breathing—no rattling sounds to indicate a problem; and circulation—her pulse was fast but not overly so.

Josh had followed her down and now held his son, talking softly to him, telling him how brave he was.

Ella felt around her head, her fingers gentle, feeling for a bump. There was nothing obvious, and when she lifted one of Brianna's translucent eyelids and shone the light in her eye, right on cue the muscle controlling the iris dilated, causing the pupil to grow smaller. The pupil of the other eye also contracted and though it wasn't a promise that there was no brain damage, Ella felt a little easier.

She opened the first-aid kit, found a small cervical collar and put it around Brianna's neck then turned her attention to her leg. No bone showing through, so it was a closed fracture of the tibia or fibula or both. Not wanting to give the child a painkiller until she knew there was no brain damage, she splinted the leg, then spoke to Brianna, calling her name, urging her to respond.

'Ella?'

It was the sweetest sound Ella had ever heard and though she couldn't lift the little girl and hug her, she leaned over and kissed her and promised her she'd be all right.

She turned her attention to Pete, asking him if anything hurt, if he had bumped his head.

'No, I'm all right. Some of the rocks slipped when we came through the tunnel and sort of carried us down, but one fell on Brianna and hurt her leg.'

Satisfied Pete was all right, Ella turned to Josh.

'Take Pete up first,' she said. 'I want to stabilise Brianna on the stretcher before we move her. If you could trail a rope then when I have her on the stretcher and up at the top of the ladder, you or one of the others can pull the stretcher through, with me following behind.'

'*You* should go first,' Josh said, and Ella knew he was anxious about the water, but she couldn't hurry Brianna's rescue and she was confident she could hold her out of the water if it kept rising.

Josh stopped arguing when she explained that, and lifted his son into his arms. He climbed the ladder, explaining to Pete he'd have to crawl, assuring him he was right behind him, playing out the rope that led back down to Ella as he went.

Harry whimpered again and Ella turned her light on him. One of his back legs was bleeding badly and he hadn't been as lucky as Brianna—his was an open fracture.

'My poor boy,' Ella said, wondering where to begin to ease his pain. She wasn't sure about dogs with head injuries but he'd need to be knocked out before she could touch his leg.

She broke open an ampoule of morphine and drew it into a syringe, working on his body weight being twice that of Brianna's. She'd just finished injecting it and had watched him put his head down in sleep when Josh called that he was through and she could follow.

'Hang on a few minutes. I'll call when I'm ready.'

She unfolded the stretcher Josh had left, fitted the sides together to make it rigid then realised there was no way she could get both the child and the dog on it. But the waters were rising fast and she couldn't leave an unconscious dog to drown. Couldn't leave Harry, who'd saved the children with his barking.

She took off her shirt, wishing she had thick overalls on, and padded the stretcher so Brianna wouldn't feel the worst of the bumps on the journey through the choke. Then she eased the stretcher under Brianna and strapped her to it, whispering all the time so the little girl knew what she was doing. Then she hauled the stretcher up the ladder behind her, found the ledge at the top, attached the rope that led through to the rescuers and tied it to the stretcher. Then she leaned into the hole and called to Josh.

'You can pull her through now,' she said, 'but gently. And make sure Nash is there when she comes out and gets her into an ambulance for a proper examination. Tell him if she has to go straight to hospital he's to get Sarah and they should both go with her so she's not afraid on her own.'

'I'm here, Ella.' Nash's voice, sounding confused, but that might just be because of the echoes of the rain and thunder and the sound of rushing water behind her in the cave. 'You're coming through right behind her. You can go to hospital with her.'

He must think she'd flipped—that the tension had got to her—and he was being kind and patient and explaining things carefully, like you did to patients who took a while to understand.

In fact, the tension hadn't got to her—not yet—but his kindness did and she had to swallow before she explained.

'No, *you* have to take care of her, Nash. Remember what we think. She's yours, too. I won't be long but I've got to get Harry out.'

She heard his curse, then angry words. Words that described her as a stupid fool, words ordering her to come right through this very minute and that someone else would go in and get the dog. In fact, he'd come through himself if she'd just get herself out of there.

'You can't come through, Nash,' she explained. 'There's already water coming through the crawl space and that's dislodging rocks on this side. Pete said it was a slide that caused Brianna's injury—we can't risk more because the tunnel could close up and with the water rising so fast there'd be no way out.'

She paused and thought she heard him swearing again, but more quietly this time, which suggested Brianna was safely through the other side and he didn't want to upset her.

'Brianna's here. She's conscious. I'm taking her up top,' he said, his voice so husky she knew how much he was hurting. Then, though she knew damn well there must be at least a dozen SES personnel around, he called out again.

'I love you, Ella,' he said, and Ella heard a cheer from the bystanders.

He loved her?

'He sure has a funny way of showing it,' she said to the unconscious Harry as she descended the ladder. She'd propped his head on a rock, but the rest of his body was now under water so somehow she had to get however many pounds of wet dog up the ladder and through the crawl space, which now resembled a storm water drain.

She took off her trousers and tied them around the dog's chest, wishing again she'd worn more clothes. Then she tied the end of the trouser legs around her waist so Harry would, hopefully, be fastened to her back when she stood up.

Well, it turned out he was fastened more to her bottom, but by pushing it out she was able to hold him there as she slowly and carefully climbed the ladder.

Water was running over the little ledge she'd thought of as a refuge, but it seemed solid enough. She pulled up the rope ladder and unfastened it, then untied Harry and removed her bra. Folding the ladder to make a kind of very flexible stretcher, she used her bra to tie him to it. Then she wrapped her trousers around his head in a makeshift helmet so his head didn't get too bashed about in transit and, grasping the ladder so she was holding it between her legs, she began to slither backwards through the water rushing down the tunnel.

Pull a couple of inches, rest, pull a couple of inches, rest.

'Do you need a rope in there?' Josh called, and though she'd have given anything to have a rope and for strong men to pull them both out, she knew if anyone else entered the space the weight could alter the dynamics of the choke and anything could happen.

'I'm getting there,' she called back. 'Just be ready to pass me a shirt as soon as you see me. I'm not coming out of this tunnel starkers for the amusement of you guys.'

But she didn't actually remember coming out of the tunnel, though someone wrapped a shirt around her shoulders and held her close and whispered more words of love, and Dennis, the vet, was there to take Harry.

It had to be Nash holding her, but he should have been with Brianna. And though Ella wanted to yell at him about it, it was too nice being held, and the things he was saying were too seductive to ignore. Once again he held her tightly against his body as they were hauled up to the top, where helping hands wrapped an oiled coat around her shoulders while Nash hustled her towards what little shelter an awning stretched out from the rescue truck provided.

'Are you hurt?' he demanded as he set her down on a folding chair, the emotion in his voice now anger, not love.

'No,' she said, though she was shivering so much she could barely get the word out.

She wrapped the coat more tightly around her shoulders and let a bit of her own anger rip.

'Where's Brianna? I asked you to stay with her.'

'Sarah's with her. Brianna knows Sarah better than she knows me, and they'd only allow one person in the ambulance. I stayed behind to drive you to the hospital, though why I keep getting tangled up in your messy life I don't know.'

'You said you loved me,' Ella reminded him. 'And my life wasn't in the least bit messy until you came back into it and ruined everything.'

She knew she was likely to burst into tears any minute so she stood up and turned away from him, heading doggedly towards her house.

'Where the hell are you going now?' Nash demanded, grabbing her and swinging her into his arms again.

'Home!' she said, but softly, because beyond the fear and concern in his face she thought she could also see the love he'd mentioned earlier.

'Stupid woman,' he said, his voice breaking. Then he bent his head and kissed her, before carrying her towards a very familiar car.

'I rode with the ambulance as far as the house and brought your car back because of the rocks, but I'll get mine out while you have a shower and we'll drive up to the city in it.'

She opened her mouth to say thank you, but he all but threw her into the car and then held his hand across her lips.

'Do not argue! Do not tell me we can't leave the town without a doctor. I do not want to hear one word of protest. This town has often been without a doctor when Mum's had trouble getting locums—they'll manage.'

He was sounding so masterful Ella decided not to argue, though she did manage to get her thank you out when he got behind the wheel.

Not that he appreciated it for he immediately began to scold her for being a stupid, impulsive idiot, first rushing through to the children without proper back-up then risking her life for a dog.

'It wasn't just any dog, it was Harry,' she reminded him, though she knew she'd have done the same for a stray.

'It was still stupid,' he grumbled, pulling up at the bottom of the steps.

The storm seemed to have abated, but the sky was still

dark and Ella realised it was close to nightfall when Nash stopped at the bottom of the steps. She opened the door of the car, but her body refused to move, adrenalin depletion leading to exhaustion.

Nash cursed again and got out to come around, but when he lifted her out, his arms were gentle and the silly words he whispered into her wet hair sounded more loving than cross.

'Next time I do this we will be married and we'll probably end up making love right here under the shower,' he told her a little later as held her under a hot shower and gently sponged her scrapes and bruises. Then he washed the mud from her hair, rinsed her off and dried her in a warm, fluffy towel, sitting her on her bed, with another towel wrapped around her, while he towelled his own body dry.

Ella looked at his body and felt an ache start in her own. She was too tired to make sense of all that was happening, and too upset about Brianna to think straight. But Nash was talking about marriage as well as love—unless she was so exhausted she was hallucinating.

Did people hallucinate voices or was hallucinating to do with sight?

She couldn't remember. All she wanted to do was lie back on the bed and go to sleep, but Brianna needed her so she had to keep going for just a little longer. Later, she could sleep and after that think about Nash.

But not thinking about Nash was hard when he was right there—dressing her now, as if she were an infant.

'Stay there!' he finally said, leaving her on the bed and striding, naked except for a towel around his waist, out the door.

She sank back on the bed, promising herself she'd only sleep for a few minutes.

She woke up in his car and knew from the bright lights they'd reached the city.

'Nash?'

He turned and smiled at her.

'Awake, are you? I can't say I'm sorry. I think I've already done my back in, carrying you from place to place. I hope you have a good worker's compensation policy.'

She smiled, because she was remembering all the nice things he'd said, and even if he was sounding gruff, she was sure he'd meant some of them.

Though perhaps he thought she'd been so dopey she wouldn't remember. Perhaps he was hoping that...

'*Do* you love me or were you just saying that?'

He sighed and ran his hand through his hair.

'I think I must do,' he said grudgingly. 'Heaven knows, I could hardly have felt the way I did when you were down in that lava tube if I didn't have some strong feelings for you.'

'Well, don't make it sound as if loving me is the worst thing that could have happened in your entire life!' Ella muttered, and he smiled, reached over and mussed her hair.

'Not quite the worst,' he whispered. 'Losing you would have been far, far worse.'

Ella felt her heart melt, though she knew this was all wrong. Hadn't they been fighting just that morning? Weren't there things that had to be sorted out between them?

Big things?

Then suddenly she remembered his absurd proposal of that morning and suspicion shot through her.

'You're not saying all of this so you can marry me to get your hands on Brianna, are you?'

Nash sighed.

'See,' he said, as if she'd just proved a point. 'You keep making it hard to love you.'

But he understood her suspicion. What had she and Meg known of love—apart from the deep and abiding love they had felt for each other?

'Ella, Brianna is yours. That's indisputable and unchangeable, whatever happens between us. Yes, I'd love to share her and share other children with you. I'd love to find out if she is Russell's daughter and love for Mum to know he left a grandchild for her, but that's up to you. I won't push you to do anything about it.'

He pulled up at a red light and turned to touch her cheek.

'I love you for you—for the gutsy kid you were, and the caring, compassionate but still gutsy adult you are now. I love it that you fight me when you think I'm wrong, and that you stand up for what you believe is right, but more than that, I love you in a way that seems to have been programmed into me. Love you not only with my heart but with my bones and flesh and nerves and—'

Ella chuckled and held his hand against her cheek.

'I get the picture,' she said softly, as the light changed and they rolled forward again.

'So, will you marry me? Soon?'

With a lot of Saturday night traffic around, Nash was watching the road so he didn't see her face when she said no, and had to wait until another red light stopped them before he could look at her.

'You meant no to the soon, didn't you? You want a court-ship, I can understand that, though I'd marry you tomorrow if I could.'

He was being far more understanding than he felt, dread hovering beneath his outward calm.

'I didn't mean, no, not soon so I could have a courtship,' Ella told him, and the dread exploded through his body. 'I meant, no, I've got stuff I have to do first.'

'What kind of stuff?'

They were arguing again.

Did he really want to marry this argumentative witch?

Yes! The answer came so swiftly he knew it was true so he took another deep breath and began again.

'Stuff?'

'Unfinished business.'

'If it's with Rick Martin, I'll kill him with my bare hands and that will sort that out,' he growled, but they were ap-proaching the entrance to City Hospital and he needed all his attention on the traffic coming in and out.

He took advantage of his staff sticker and parked reasonably close to the emergency entrance then came around the car to help Ella out.

As she stood up he drew her close and held her.

'It's not Rick Martin,' she whispered against his neck, 'and it's nothing bad, just something I have to do before I can move on. Once it's done, I'll need a little time.'

For what? he wanted to yell, but she'd lifted her face and he saw the purple shadows beneath her lovely eyes and knew he'd give her all the time she wanted.

If it killed him!

Which it probably would, he decided minutes later when the gentle kiss she'd pressed on his lips had fired his senses and had his body demanding satisfaction.

'Come on. Let's find the kid!' he growled, dragging Ella inside before he was tempted to drag her into the bushes. 'I sent word with the ambos she was to be treated as priority but Saturday nights they might think knife wounds rate higher.'

But once inside they found Brianna had indeed been treated as a priority and was sporting a bright orange cast on her leg.

'Sarah chose the colour,' she explained, her hand clinging to Sarah's as if the older woman was her lifeline. 'Because they made me very sleepy with some medicine and I couldn't talk. But Sarah knows I like orange best.'

Ella kissed her niece, then kissed Sarah and thanked her, her voice breaking as she said it, while Nash was quizzing the nurse in the curtained alcove, demanding to know if they'd done skull X-rays and brain scans.

'Of course we have, Dr McLaren,' the nurse assured him. 'She's fine. In fact, Doctor said she could go home. The X-rays are all here. You can look at them yourself.'

'It was only my leg got hurt, not my head,' Brianna told Nash, and he came forward, and bent and kissed her.

'I'm very glad about that,' he said. 'OK, family, let's go home.'

Sarah smiled at him.

'It feels like that, doesn't it?' she said quietly. 'Like we're a family now.'

Ella heard the words and knew the time had come to talk to Sarah.

'I need coffee,' she said. 'Let's leave Nash to sort out the discharge while we get some to drink on the way home.'

Sarah followed her out of the alcove but Ella waited until they were at the coffee-machine before she spoke.

'This isn't going to be easy to say and I really hope you don't get upset, but Nash saw a resemblance between you and Brianna and since he pointed it out I've wondered, too.'

She took Sarah's hand and looked into her eyes.

'Meg never said who Brianna's father was, but the one thing she was adamant about was that Brianna grow up in Edenvale. There was stuff she wanted to do first—we both wanted to do—and I think once that was out of the way, she'd have told you.'

The words came out in a rush and Ella studied Sarah's face, wondering if she'd understood, then Sarah smiled, a smile so radiant Ella knew she had.

Sarah leaned forward and kissed her cheek.

'I've often wondered myself,' she said. 'I see both the boys in her, Russell especially, but I didn't want to hope—or to upset you by talking about it.'

They hugged, and Ella suspected Sarah was crying—she certainly was.

'What happened to the coffee?'

Nash, with Brianna in his arms, was right behind them, and Ella dragged in some replenishing air and turned her attention to the job at hand, while Sarah hugged her son, and the little girl who just might be her grandchild.

CHAPTER TWELVE

IT WAS a week later—though it seemed a month as Brianna hadn't been able to go to preschool and Ella had taken time off work to keep her occupied. Whenever she'd had a spare minute she'd been working on the figures, working out interest and percentages and things she'd never understood. So she'd barely seen Nash except to hide her papers and growl that she was busy—until today, when everything was done and they were together, being domestic and decorating the tree.

Brianna was directing operations when Sarah came in through the kitchen door, calling out a greeting as she came.

'In the sitting room,' Ella called to her. 'We're putting the finishing touches to the tree.'

Sarah whirled into the room, hugged Ella and waved to Nash, who was on a ladder, putting the star on the top.

'Two Christmas miracles!' Sarah announced in a joyous tone. 'You know how we get Saturday mail deliveries this close to Christmas. Well, the mail's just come and I heard the postman's bike, but I'd finally remembered where I put that box of Russell's stuff so I was delving into it and didn't go out immediately, but when I did, what do you think I found?'

She waved a letter in the air.

'This!'

'And what is this?' Nash enquired politely, though he was beginning to wonder if there weren't too many women in his life right now. Not that he'd want to do without Ella—or his mother, come to that. Or Brianna, whose warm hugs and kisses stole his breath. And, really, Mrs Carter did the best bacon and eggs—

'It's a cheque and a letter saying the cheque's for me and

there's no mistake and to please accept it in the spirit in which it has been given. It does say that if I don't want all of it, I can always give some to the appeal for a new ambulance building, but nothing else about where it came from or why.'

'What kind of cheque?' Nash asked, immediately suspicious.

'A bank cheque,' his mother said, 'so you can't tell who sent it, except what bank and the bank which issued it won't tell because that's the point of bank cheques.'

Nash sighed. It had to do with wiring, he was sure, that men and women were so different.

'I meant how much—is it a big cheque or small one?'

His mother beamed.

'Big! Very big!' She passed it up to him and he nearly fell off the ladder, counting the five figures that made it more than a small gift from someone who'd forgotten to include a card.

'And that's not all.'

Nash was still pondering the cheque, wondering just what the catch was, when his mother flourished a small bottle that she'd had in her other hand.

'I found Russell's appendix! Remember when he had it out and insisted we keep the horrible thing? Well, when I was clearing out his room, I thought how adamant he'd been and I couldn't bring myself to throw it out.'

Nash stared at her. It had to be more than different wiring that women were so unfathomable, but Ella seemed to understand. In fact, she seemed to think it equally amazing for she was hugging his mother and the pair were now dancing round and round the room.

Then they stopped, and she looked up at him.

'It means you and your mother won't have to be tested. The scientists should be able to get enough DNA material from the appendix. Though maybe the preservative it's been in might have contaminated it.'

Nash looked at her. The appendix might mean he and his mother didn't need to give blood or some other sample, but it didn't affect Ella, yet she'd reacted to that, not the money. Perhaps she didn't realise how much money was involved.

He climbed down the ladder and showed her the cheque.

'That's nice,' she said, and turned to take the scissors away from Brianna.

Mrs Carter came in before he could question Ella's reaction, holding an identical letter and a small piece of paper—cheque size.

'I've got this cheque,' she said faintly. 'From out of nowhere this money comes, and the letter says it's for me and legal and all.'

His mother checked the letter and showed Mrs Carter hers, but Ella didn't react at all.

Why wasn't she surprised?

Nash left the room, going out on to the veranda before pulling his mobile out of his pocket. He phoned Bob.

'Have you had a windfall in the mail this morning?' he asked his old friend.

'No such luck,' Bob told him, 'but Dad phoned to say they'd got a cheque in the mail and he reckons half the people in the retirement place where he lives have got them as well, all for different amounts and with no explanation other than the money is theirs to do with as they wish, though the letter apparently mentions something about a new ambulance building if they want to make a donation.'

'Stuff!' Nash muttered, and when Bob asked him what he meant, Nash apologised and hung up. Ella had had 'stuff' to do before they could get married, and Meg had had 'stuff' to do—'stuff' she'd wanted done before she brought Brianna back to Edenvale.

Add to that the fact Ella was passionate about getting the town a second ambulance—which meant putting up a new building.

He almost smiled at the temerity of her suggestion that some people might want to make a donation...

All the photocopying and the furtive hiding of papers—it was all falling into place. But how the hell had she got the money—and with her maths skills worked out interest? The cheque his mother had received was way more than the family had lost in the co-op failure.

He phoned three more people he knew who'd had shares in the co-op before deciding he was right, then he headed straight for Ella's bedroom. She kept the papers in a battered old briefcase. He knew because he'd seen her hide them in it.

It was under the bed, and he hauled it out and opened it up, spilling the papers onto the bed and spreading them with his hand, seeing the lists of names and the painful crossings-out all through the figures.

Of all the stupid, determined, stiff-necked-with-pride women...

'You're in my room!'

'I should be living here—or you in my room,' he growled, turning to face her and crossing his arms. 'Stuff! This is the stuff you've been doing? Paying back not only the money your father lost but interest—though how you managed to work out the compound interest on individual amounts over twelve years, I wouldn't know.'

'I didn't,' she said in a very small voice, looking down at her toes. 'I tried, I really did, but in the end it was too much so I found out the highest interest rates banks had paid in the last twelve years, and multiplied that percentage of the money by twelve and added it on.'

She looked up, hazel eyes pleading for his understanding.

'Do you think I cheated them of much?'

Nash shook his head. He couldn't speak for the lump that had formed in his throat, so he stepped towards her and took her in his arms.

'Oh, Ella,' he whispered, when he'd swallowed hard a couple of times. 'You didn't have to do this, sweetheart. It was your father's debt, not yours. It was never yours.'

'Mine and Meg's,' she corrected him, leaning against his body as if she really needed his support. 'It was Meg's insurance that made it possible to pay the interest as well. When we first decided and started saving, we thought we'd just pay back the amount people lost, but when Meg died, well, her insurance should have gone to Brianna, but she'd made a will leaving it to me and saying I knew what I had to do with it, so it meant I had to be sure of making a good life for Brianna without using the insurance money, which was why I wanted to buy the practice if someone would lend me enough, but then the interest made it all so hard to work out.'

He held her tight, his heart so full of love for this generous, mixed-up, wonderful woman it was a wonder it could still keep beating.

Then she pushed away from him and said, 'You won't tell, will you? We wanted to do it but so no one would know. And I didn't think people would mind that I reminded them about the ambulance building.'

He kissed her because once again he couldn't speak, then he remembered something else. He tilted her head and looked down into her eyes.

'OK,' he said. 'Now, you tell me this. Back when you said you couldn't marry me soon, you said it was because you had stuff to do—which I'm assuming is now done—and then time for something else. What something else?'

She smiled at him.

'I wanted to have time to save up for a wedding dress,' she whispered, her eyes clouding with tears. 'I know you'll think that's stupid and pathetic and "girly", like you called me once before, but I've worn cast-offs and secondhand clothes for so long, I'd like something new to wear—something to make you proud of me.'

He hugged her tight.

'I could never be more proud of you than I am right now,' he whispered, 'but I'm damned if I'll let your pride put off our wedding any longer. Next weekend we'll go to town and you'll pick out the wedding dress of your dreams and I'll be paying for it, Ella Marsden—no argument!'

Ella didn't argue. She just snuggled back into his arms, certain she'd finally come home to Edenvale.

Experience the magic of Christmas, past and present...

Christmas Brides

Don't miss this special holiday volume — two captivating love stories set in very different times.

THE GREEK'S CHRISTMAS BRIDE
by Lucy Monroe
Modern Romance

Aristide Kouros has no memory of life with his beautiful wife Eden. Though she's heartbroken he does not remember their passion for each other, Eden still loves her husband. But what secret is she hiding that might bind Aristide to her forever – whether he remembers her or not?

MOONLIGHT AND MISTLETOE
by Louise Allen
Historical Romance – Regency

From her first night in her new home in a charming English village, Hester is plagued by intrusive "hauntings." With the help of her handsome neighbour, the Earl of Buckland, she sets out to discover the mystery behind the frightful encounters – while fighting her own fear of falling in love with the earl.

On sale 4th November 2005

Celebrate Christmas with the Fortunes!

Enjoy three classic stories with the Fortunes—a family whose Christmas legacy is greater than mere riches.

ANGEL BABY by Lisa Jackson
Lesley Bastian is so grateful to Chase Fortune for delivering her baby – but trying to penetrate the walls around Chase's heart is almost as challenging as motherhood!

A HOME FOR CHRISTMAS by Barbara Boswell
As CEO of a major corporation, Ryder Fortune has little time for romance – until his assistant Joanna Chandler works her way into his hardened heart…

THE CHRISTMAS CHILD by Linda Turner
Naomi Windsong's little girl is missing and only Hunter Fortune can find her. But will time prove to be Hunter's greatest enemy – and love his greatest challenge?

THE FORTUNES
The price of privilege—the power of family.

On sale 18th November 2005

FREE

4 BOOKS AND A SURPRISE GIFT!

We would like to take this opportunity to thank you for reading this Mills & Boon® book by offering you the chance to take FOUR more specially selected titles from the Medical Romance™ series absolutely FREE! We're also making this offer to introduce you to the benefits of the Reader Service™—

- ★ **FREE home delivery**
- ★ **FREE gifts and competitions**
- ★ **FREE monthly Newsletter**
- ★ **Books available before they're in the shops**
- ★ **Exclusive Reader Service offers**

Accepting these FREE books and gift places you under no obligation to buy; you may cancel at any time, even after receiving your free shipment. Simply complete your details below and return the entire page to the address below. You don't even need a stamp!

YES! Please send me 4 free Medical Romance books and a surprise gift. I understand that unless you hear from me, I will receive 6 superb new titles every month for just £2.75 each, postage and packing free. I am under no obligation to purchase any books and may cancel my subscription at any time. The free books and gift will be mine to keep in any case.

M5ZEE

Ms/Mrs/Miss/Mr..Initials ....
BLOCK CAPITALS PLEASE

Surname ....

Address ....

....

....Postcode ....

Send this whole page to:
The Reader Service, FREEPOST CN81, Croydon, CR9 3WZ

Offer valid in UK only and is not available to current Reader Service™subscribers to this series. Overseas and Eire please write for details. We reserve the right to refuse an application and applicants must be aged 18 years or over. Only one application per household. Terms and prices subject to change without notice. Offer expires 28th February 2006. As a result of this application, you may receive offers from Harlequin Mills & Boon and other carefully selected companies. If you would prefer not to share in this opportunity please write to The Data Manager at PO Box 676, Richmond, TW9 1WU.

Mills & Boon® is a registered trademark owned by Harlequin Mills & Boon Limited.
Medical Romance™ is being used as a trademark. The Reader Service™ is being used as a trademark.